In USA Today bestselling author Janice Maynard's sweet and sexy series, three childhood friends with a shared passion for the Outlander novels and TV show decide to travel to Scotland looking for adventure—and their very own Highland heroes...

McKenzie Taylor is high maintenance when it comes to fashion, but when it comes to travel, the socialite prefers privacy to parties, and her own space to hotels. After she and her friends arrive in Scotland and split up to pursue their own adventures, she rents a small cottage on the Isle of Skye. On day two, she crashes her rental car. But a hero emerges from the mist to rescue her. He's handsome, earthy, funny, and before long is making her feel desirable, not mention desirous. There's just one problem: McKenzie's Highland dreamboat is a motorcycle riding American.

Finley Craig knows his cute new tourist friend is stubbornly set on falling for a Scotsman. But he's just as set on her falling for him. So he plans to give her a taste of what she thinks she wants. Because Finley suspects McKenzie isn't as shallow as she appears. And in the process of surrounding her with his hand-picked suitors, she may just decide that American-made is best—especially when she and Finley are rained in together over one long, delicious, and very adventurous weekend...

Books by Janice Maynard

Kilted Heroes
Hot for the Scot
Scot of My Dreams
Not Quite a Scot

Published by Kensington Publishing Corporation

Not Quite A Scot

Kilted Heroes

Janice Maynard

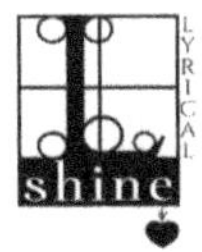

LYRICAL PRESS
Kensington Publishing Corp.
www.kensingtonbooks.com

Lyrical Press books are published by
Kensington Publishing Corp. 119 West 40th Street New York, NY 10018

All Kensington titles, imprints, and distributed lines are available at special quantity discounts for bulk purchases for sales promotion, premiums, fund-raising, and educational or institutional use.

Special book excerpts or customized printings can also be created to fit specific needs. For details, write or phone the office of the Kensington Special Sales Manager:
Kensington Publishing Corp.
119 West 40th Street
New York, NY 10018
Attn. Special Sales Department. Phone: 1-800-221-2647.

First Electronic Edition: November 2016
eISBN-13: 978-1-60183-629-8
eISBN-10: 1-60183-629-5

First Print Edition: November 2016
ISBN-13: 978-1-60183-630-4
ISBN-10: 1-60183-630-9

Printed in the United States of America

For anyone who has ever wanted to jet off or sail away to the other side of the globe… I give you Scotland: her mystery, her history, her bold independence. May her rugged Highlands remain unspoiled and her people continue to march to the tune of a different piper…

Chapter 1

Headed for Inverness on the East Coast Train…

Scotland. The Highlands. Purple heather. Northern lights. Men in kilts. I was too excited to sleep. I might have made this journey on my own long ago. Instead, I had waited until the moment was right. The wrong companions could ruin even the most exotic trip. Luckily, I'd known the two women traveling with me since we were all in diapers.

Hayley—whose mother ran the in-home daycare where my friends and I first met as toddlers—taught third grade. She was organized, earnest, and one of the most caring people I'd ever known. It pleased me to see her so happy. She practically vibrated with enthusiasm.

After the long flight from Atlanta to Heathrow—and a brief night of sleep in a nondescript hotel room—the three of us were now sitting in motor coach–style seats on either side of a small rectangular table. The train racketed along at high speeds, stopping now and again to drop off and pick up passengers as we whizzed through the countryside. Hayley had finished her tea and was poring over one of the guidebooks she'd brought along.

Willow, on the other hand, brooded loudly, if such a thing were possible. I suspected her cranky attitude was a cover for very real nerves. She had never traveled farther than a few hundred miles from the Peach State. This was a big step for her, not only because of transportation firsts, but because she'd had to leave her business behind.

The salon she co-owned, *Hair Essentials,* was the product of blood, sweat, and tears. Willow's history was neither as privileged as mine nor as stable as Hayley's. Yet somehow, our cynical friend had managed to find her own path, and a successful one at that.

I stifled an unexpected yawn, swamped by a wave of fatigue. Despite the collection of stamps in my passport, I'd never mastered the art of crossing time zones unscathed.

Willow and I had been squabbling half-heartedly for the last hour. As if sensing that I was losing my steam, she half turned in her seat and glared at me. "Jamie Fraser is a fictional character," she said. "Like Harry Potter or Jason Bourne. You're not going to find him wandering around the Scottish Highlands waiting to sweep you off your feet."

I glared right back at her. "I *know* that. I'm not delusional. But at least I have a whimsical soul. You wouldn't know a romantic moment if it smacked you in the face."

We were in the midst of an ongoing argument that neither of us was going to win. I knew the Harry Potter reference was a deliberate jab at me. Though my travel companions had moaned, I'd awakened them early enough this morning to make it to King's Cross Station for photographs and retail therapy. After all, it wasn't every day I had a chance to get my picture taken at the famous Platform 9 ¾.

By the time I scoured the handkerchief-sized gift shop and braved the line of tourists posing for the platform picture, we'd had mere minutes to make our noon departure. It was worth the mad scramble. I considered J. K. Rowling one of the wonders of the modern world.

Willow wasn't really miffed about my Harry Potter obsession. She was scared…scared that we three were embarking on an outlandish adventure sure to disappoint us in the end. I could see it in her wary gaze. Life—and probably men as well—had not been kind to her.

Hayley looked at Willow and me with hurt, puppy dog eyes, as if stunned we could be at odds in the midst of this great adventure. "You're both jet-lagged," she said. "If you're not going to enjoy the trip, at least get some sleep so you won't be grumpy when we get to Inverness. I'm tired of listening to both of you."

Willow and I tabled our squabbles in favor of closing our eyes. Now the sensation of motion intensified. The train raced along, offering tantalizing glimpses of the countryside each time I peeked. Though I had spent a week in Edinburgh several years ago, this was my first chance to venture north. I had told Willow and Hayley that a recent bequest from my grandmother's estate prompted our bucket list trip, but in truth, I'd been planning this pilgrimage for some time.

I was trying to make up for the decade and a half when my childhood friends and I lost touch. Though Hayley's mom had eventually caught up with most of her daycare graduates via Facebook, in the years before that, little more than Christmas cards kept the connection alive between my friends and me.

Our lives had taken far different paths. Hayley was firmly middle-class America with two loving parents and a conventional job. Willow, on the other hand, didn't talk much about her past. Her father had walked out right about the time my parents pulled me from public school and enrolled me in an elite academy. Willow and her mom had been forced to rely on the kindness of relatives who lived on the opposite side of the city.

Despite our differences and the years we spent apart, we were closer now than ever, partly because of a shared obsession, albeit a harmless one. We were all three madly enamored with Diana Gabaldon's *Outlander* books, and more recently, the TV series. We spent hours critiquing the first season of the show, deciding that although nothing could compare to the actual book, the producers and directors and cast had done a bang-up job of bringing Claire Randall and Jamie Fraser to life.

Somewhere, somehow, in the midst of a sleepless spring night when my hormones were raging and my good sense waning, I had seized on the idea that Hayley and Willow and I should travel to Scotland and seek out our own Outlander-style adventures, preferably with a kilt-clad hero involved.

I knew my plan was farfetched. Guys like the fictional Jamie Fraser, particularly in the twenty-first century, were few and far between. I'd dated my share of losers. Kissing frogs was a rite of passage for millennials.

In my personal experience, though, American men tended to fall into three categories: mama's boys who wanted another woman to take care of them; high-powered workaholics who didn't need or care about real relationships; and last but not least, a large group of genuinely nice guys who would make great boyfriend or husband material, but didn't get my heart (or anywhere else) all fizzy.

Still, I couldn't give up hope that somewhere out there was the one man who was my soul mate. I didn't actually share that belief with my friends for several reasons. Hayley lived like a nun, and Willow was too much of a hard-ass to believe in fairytale romance. Or if she *did* believe in it, she sure as heck wouldn't admit to something so *girly*.

My goal for this trip was to get away from everything that pigeonholed me back in the States. I lived mostly in Atlanta, but my parents had a penthouse apartment in New York and a ski chalet in St. Moritz. I was the epitome of the poor little rich girl. I knew my last nanny better than I knew my own mother.

I wasn't complaining. Not at all. Nobody ever said life was fair. Since I'd never had to clip coupons or worry about my car being repossessed, I suppose it made cosmic sense that the average American family wasn't something I would ever have. No Monopoly games around the kitchen table. No making s'mores over a summer campfire. No irritating siblings to steal the attention from me.

Hayley and Willow were the closest thing to sisters I would ever have. I felt more than a little guilty that I had bludgeoned them into making this trip. Even though I paid for the first class airfare and train tickets, the two of them were still going to be out of pocket for lodging and meals.

I wished they would let me cover that, too, but Hayley had pulled me aside months ago and pointed out that she and Willow needed to feel invested in this adventure and not entirely beholden to me. Like Claire Randall, the gutsy heroine of *Outlander*, we were supposed be bold and independent. In the process, perhaps we might stumble upon our own gorgeous, chivalrous, modern-day Highlanders.

Hayley believed it could happen. Willow would probably work hard to make sure it *didn't* happen. And as for me…well, I as far as I was concerned, it was a pleasant daydream.

My repeated yawns were rubbing off on Willow. She pinched the bridge of her nose. "Tell me again why we didn't fly straight to Inverness?"

"You know why," Hayley said. She opened her notebook. "We agreed that since we can't actually go back in time like Claire does in *Outlander*, this train journey will be symbolic of our desire to go off the grid for a month. No cell phones. No Internet. No Facebook. No Twitter. You agreed, Willow."

"Under duress," she muttered.

I snickered. "You're bitchy when you're tired."

"And you're even more annoying than usual," Willow drawled.

Usually, I loved a good argument. At the moment, though, I was not at my best. After a warning glance from Hayley, I pretended to sleep again. Maybe that would keep me out of trouble.

This train ride had turned me inside out. I was flooded with all sorts of feelings. The fact that my two best friends had followed along with my mad scheme humbled me. I would be absolutely devastated if either of them ended up getting hurt, either physically or emotionally.

It wasn't too late to back out. One word from me and I felt sure either or both of my friends would agree to a new course of action, one where we stuck together as a team. Why had *safe* seemed like such a dirty word?

Our plan was to remain together tonight at the hotel adjacent to the train station in Inverness. Then tomorrow morning, we would all three go our separate ways. My stomach clenched and my chest tightened. Whatever happened after that would be all my fault.

Hayley tapped the notebook where she had underlined the final piece of our plan. "And remember—every night at nine o'clock, or as close as we can make it, we'll turn on our phones and check for any emergency messages from each other."

Willow nodded. "I won't forget." I sensed that she was as worried about Hayley as I was. Willow had street smarts, but our schoolteacher friend exhibited a naïve streak a mile wide.

The odd thing was, Willow and I were probably the two with the most in common. Which sounded ridiculous given the circumstances of our upbringing. But it was true.

Hayley possessed the wide-eyed wonder of a child and a nonchalant certainty that people were basically nice and sweet and accommodating. Lord help us if she ever found out that wasn't true.

Then there was Willow: hard-working, gruff Willow. Rough around the edges. Abnormally cautious when it came to money. Almost always expecting the worst. I'm sure she would hoot at the comparison, but she and I shared a similar outlook. Neither of us wanted to depend on anyone else for our happiness and our security.

Willow had coped with poverty and a dysfunctional family. The hand I'd been dealt included too much money and parents who barely acknowledged my existence. I'd long since given up trying to win their approval.

Even if I could go out tomorrow, marry a Wall Street banker, and pop out two point five kids, it still wouldn't be enough. My father's career engulfed him. My mother's vanity and narcissism absorbed her.

Thank God I had two such amazing human beings for friends. I loved both with a raw intensity that would probably astonish each of them in different ways. With seven years of adult friendship under our belts to bolster our childhood memories, I would never let them go. Not the recollections of the past, and certainly not the women themselves.

Hayley and Willow and I were the same age. At the moment, though, I felt the sole burden of responsibility. This entire Outlander scheme was *my* idea. If it failed, I'd be to blame. If it succeeded, even on a superficial level, we'd have a thrilling month ahead.

Despite the panic and the second thoughts, the prospect was exhilarating. Was there a Jamie out there for me? A strong, chivalrous Scotsman who would fight for me and keep me warm at night?

I closed my eyes and tried to conjure up his face.

Inverness couldn't get here soon enough…

Chapter 2

We arrived at our destination just after eight. I had booked us into a lovely old hotel adjacent to the train station, which was a good thing, because I was fading fast. Hayley and Willow looked as bad as I felt.

I ushered them inside, and we dumped all our bags in a small sitting area. Check-in took no time at all. The clerk was friendly and efficient. Soon, we were crammed into the tiny elevator heading upward, though the trip was agonizingly slow.

Our room consisted of two single beds and barely enough space for a rollaway cot. Hayley volunteered for the cot immediately. That might have been a self-sacrificing offer on her part. More likely, she knew nothing would keep her from conking out. It was easy to see that all three of us were hitting bottom. For the past few weeks we'd been buoyed by excitement and adrenaline. Now we were too tired to care about *Outlander* or Scotland or even food.

My two roomies clearly agreed with me, though none of us said a word as we got ready for bed. I was the one to turn out the lights. The glow from a streetlight outside our window illuminated the room even with the drapes closed. "I'm glad you both came with me," I said. I wish I could make them see how momentous this was, how utterly wonderful.

"Me, too," Hayley said, yawning and punching her thin pillow into a more comfortable contour.

Willow groaned aloud. "I'm sorry I was in a bad mood earlier. I really am excited. But are we absolutely sure we want to split up?"

There was the hard question. We had fleshed out this idea as a team. Clearly, I wasn't the only one experiencing doubts.

Hayley spoke up before I could say anything. "We have to," she said firmly. "If we're really going to be on the lookout for our own Scottish heroes, we need to be independent. A cluster of three women isn't likely to attract the attention of an available Scotsman."

I laughed out loud in spite of my fatigue. "Unless he's into ménage à trois."

Hayley gave me a schoolmarm look. With her face washed clean and her jammies on, she looked almost like a teenager. "Your math skills suck," she said. "And I don't know the French word for four. Go to sleep. We don't have to say goodbye yet."

* * * ****

The next morning, I clung desperately to my positive attitude. I'd wanted so badly for everything to be perfect for Hayley and Willow. I traveled frequently, but this was the first big trip either of them had ever made. Why did the weather have to be so depressingly… *Scottish*?

I didn't mind rainy days as a rule. There was something soothing about a gentle, steady downpour. But not now. It didn't seem fair to my travel companions *or* to the Highlands. Not when first impressions were so important. I wanted my friends to have the time of their lives. So far, the only thing to see was a blanket of grey mist covering the city.

Over breakfast, I tried to keep the conversation going. We were a quiet bunch. I sensed that anticipation had taken a backseat to reluctance and maybe even dread. Hayley looked downright scared. Willow was harder to read.

Though I had nothing to feel guilty about, I squirmed inwardly. Should I be the one to rewrite our game plan? After all, I'd initiated the trip. Here in the confines of the hotel, we were safe. And together. What had seemed like a lark back in the States suddenly felt astonishingly real.

A month was a heck of a long time. Did I dare send my two little chicks out into the world without me?

My agitation stole my appetite, though I stuffed down bacon and eggs. One thing I had learned over the years while traveling in remote sections of the world was to eat when the chance arose. You never knew when the next meal would come around.

Hayley, God love her, insisted on trying the haggis. Willow pretended to gag theatrically. I smiled. I knew that sheep organs mixed with oatmeal weren't my cup of tea. And speaking of tea…I lifted a hand and waved for the server. After requesting a fresh pot of hot water, I smeared raspberry marmalade on toast and ate it along with my final cup of Earl Grey.

When we had finished our meal, I reached into my big leather tote and held out three small tissue-wrapped objects. "Pick one," I said. The roomy, turquoise Kate Spade bag had been a gift from my grandma on my twenty-first birthday. Grammy would have approved of this trip.

Willow and Hayley chose at the same moment. With a nod from me, they unwrapped the gifts. Inside each was a small oval box, perhaps two or three inches across and an inch deep. The lid was inscribed with Celtic symbols. I really hoped they liked them.

"It's beautiful," Hayley said.

Willow stared at hers. "This is an antique, Mac. Must have been wickedly expensive."

I waved a hand. "They're snuffboxes. I found them on eBay. Sterling silver and ram's horn. Aren't they cool? Even women dipped tobacco back in the day."

Hayley ran a finger over the engraving on hers. "I love it. But I know you don't expect me to take up dipping."

"Of course not. These are for us to collect mementos. Anything that touches our souls or stirs our imaginations. Little bits and pieces to remind us of our trip, so that in the weeks and months to come, we can open the boxes and remember Scotland."

"It's a lovely idea," Hayley said.

Willow nodded. "Thanks, McKenzie. I have no idea what I'll find, but I'll keep my eyes open."

Their genuine pleasure reassured me. I might have fudged a bit when Willow protested. The boxes *had* been pricey. After all, they were very old and in mint condition. I knew the moment I saw them they were the perfect gift for the two friends who had given me so much.

A short time later, we stood out on the walk, huddled beneath an overhang. I had ordered a cab to take me to the car rental place. Soon I would be on my way to the Isle of Skye.

Willow and Hayley clutched bus schedules in their hands. Willow had made arrangements to stay in the general Inverness area but in a youth hostel. Hayley was headed south for a village on the shores of Loch Ness.

Suddenly, emotion closed my throat.

Hayley voiced the words I didn't speak. "Be safe," she said.

Willow nodded. "And don't do anything stupid."

My cab pulled up at the curb. I gave the driver a grateful smile as he loaded my bags into the trunk. When it was time to step into the car, I hesitated. Glancing over my shoulder, I took one last look at my friends.

"Remember Claire," I said. "Be brave." Because I was on the verge of stupid, sentimental tears, I got in the car and gave the driver the go-ahead.

As the vehicle started to move off down the street, I twisted in my seat and peered out the back windshield.

While I watched, a bus pulled up in front of the hotel. I saw Willow pick up her backpack and suitcase and hug Hayley. By the time she boarded, my cab turned a corner and I lost sight of the hotel entirely.

A fluttery sense of panic engulfed me. How could I leave dear Hayley all alone? I tapped the driver on the shoulder. "Would you mind to go back around the block?" I asked. "I want to make sure my friend gets picked up."

The man nodded, unfazed, as if accustomed to the eccentricities of tourists. By the time we made it back to the hotel, no one stood in the street. In the distance, a different bus, not Willow's, trundled down the pavement.

"Okay," I said. "I guess everything's fine."

I sat back in my seat, feeling a definite sense of anticlimax. From here on out, I was on my own. I was counting on Scotland to entertain and inspire me. Anything else would be gravy.

Chapter 3

Hindsight is 20/20. I'd heard my grandmother spout that maxim a hundred times while I was growing up—usually in the context of some mischief I'd created. She was always trying to show me the error of my ways…to teach me how to look before I leaped. Sadly, she was gone now, and I was still the same impulsive, leap-before-you-look kind of woman.

Today was a case in point. After leaving my two friends in Inverness, I should have driven immediately to my destination and settled in. Privacy was important to me…that, and the space to breathe. Instead of booking a hotel somewhere, I'd chosen to rent a small cottage on the Isle of Skye for the entire month.

My goal, other than the only-half-serious one of finding a hunky Scotsman, was to polish my photography skills. I was a good amateur, but I wanted to take things a step farther…maybe even snag a gallery exhibition of my work.

It's not like I needed the money. Even if no one bought a single print, it would be okay—disappointing, but okay. I just wanted to prove to myself that I was good at something other than being McKenzie Taylor.

The trip from Inverness to the charming town of Portree on Skye was two and a half hours. Even on a rainy day. I should have arrived well before dinner. That timeline, however, assumed I was a straight-from-A-to-B kind of person, which I wasn't.

First off, I lingered in Inverness. Tucked away on a side street, I found a secondhand bookstore I'd read about. Leakey's was housed in an old church with floor to ceiling shelves and the aroma of aging paper and fresh-baked scones. Thousands of books, mostly out-of-print, were crammed into every nook and corner. I lost myself in the crowded aisles.

Though I could easily have left with a dozen volumes, I limited my purchase to only three: a history of the Highlands published in the late 1800s, a coffee table book of Highland photographs and essays and a book of recipes that looked interesting. I wasn't a gourmet cook, but I did like to putter in the kitchen. Perhaps I would perfect a dish or two while here in Scotland.

By the time I finished shopping, my stomach growled. I lingered in the store's coffee shop corner for a bowl of soup. Then by early afternoon, I was on my way.

Cloudy days might be dismal to some travelers, but for a would-be photographer, the weather was perfect, especially since the rain had dwindled to a non-threatening mist. The light was amazing, the scenery even more so. I found myself stopping every couple of miles to take shots of moody lochs and raw, windswept hills.

I'd splurged before leaving home and bought a brand new, high-end digital SLR camera. With the online manual and my own fairly extensive experience with the latest photo editing software, I was convinced I'd be able to satisfy my artistic ambitions.

Unfortunately, my fascination with the Scottish countryside, particularly as seen through the lens of my new camera, made me lose track of time. By the time I finally made it out to the island of Skye and up to the tiny town of Portree, I was starving again. Though I was eager to find my rental house, I stopped for a late dinner of sautéed scallops, warm, fresh-baked bread, and a single glass of perfectly chilled Pinot Grigio. I knew my accommodations would not be stocked with groceries. That would be up to me.

By the time I was done eating, the light had begun to fade. I wasn't too worried. I'd been given good directions, and though it *had* been some time since I'd driven on the left side of the road, after today's trip, it was coming back to me.

Once again behind the wheel of my rental car, I headed north up the hill and out of town. Soon, dwellings were fewer and far between, and I was out on my own. A shiver of unease snaked up my spine. "Don't be silly," I said out loud, giving myself a pep talk. I couldn't be more than a couple of miles from my destination.

Though I was driving slowly, it was difficult to make out signposts until I was practically on top of them. Twice, I backed up carefully to see if I had missed my turn-off. Here was a situation where it would have been nice to have a passenger to navigate while I concentrated on the road.

My pulse picked up speed in inverse proportion to the pace at which the car now crawled. I wanted to pull over and consult my map, but the road was narrow. What if someone came flying over a small rise and rear-ended me?

Despite my many travels, I was not at my best. Every shadow in the dark seemed threatening. Losing patience, I pressed down on the accelerator. *What's the worst that could happen?* If I passed my turn-off, all I had to do was back up or turn around.

As I sailed along, cocooned in the relative naiveté of my plan, some kind of small animal darted out in front of me. Its frantic eyes glowed momentarily in the beam of my headlights. "Hell's bells!" I jerked the wheel to keep from hitting the creature and promptly ended up in a ditch.

The impact jarred everything from my teeth to my tailbone. I shut off the engine and sucked in great gulps of oxygen, trying not to cry.

The car was tilted at a forty-five-degree angle. Fortunately, my side was up and not down. Though I knew instinctively it would do no good, I carefully shifted from park into drive and gave it some gas. Nothing happened. Unless I missed my guess, I had at least two wheels not making contact with anything at all. Even more worrisome was the loud noise that had accompanied my precipitous stop. I was very much afraid I had broken an axle.

In the grand scheme of things, that was no big deal. I had signed off on the extra insurance at the rental company. Even if *this* car was not drivable, I would surely be able to get a replacement in the morning.

That, however, was cold comfort at the moment. It wasn't as if I could call Triple A for a tow. I was well and truly stuck.

Though I might eventually be reduced to sleeping in my disabled car, I had to do something in the meantime. I was wearing the same white pantsuit I had traveled in yesterday, with a clean silk tank top underneath. The night was cool but not uncomfortably so. My jacket was long-sleeved, so I was fine for the moment.

Thankful for the yoga lessons I had taken continually since my junior year in high school, I lowered the window and levered myself up and out of the vehicle. I knew I couldn't be far from the ocean. In daylight I could probably see it from where I stood.

Water didn't scare me. I did, however, have a healthy fear of plunging over a cliff. For the first time it occurred to me that the wise thing to have done was book a hotel room in Portree and make this trip tomorrow morning.

With keys in hand, I went to the rear of the vehicle and tried to open the trunk. The electronic button on the key fob produced no results. Next, I inserted the key and tried to open it the old-fashioned way. No luck.

It seemed as if the frame had bent, just enough to keep me out of my belongings. I was deeply thankful that I had put my purse and carry-on up front with me. At least I had something.

Standing in the middle of the road, I pondered my next move. Willow and Hayley and I had agreed not to use technology for the next month except in an emergency. This definitely qualified. When I pulled out my phone and powered it on, I saw only a single bar. Even that small glimmer of positivity went in and out.

I tried anyway, choosing to call the restaurant where I had dined not long ago. I'd found the phone number on my credit card receipt. Portree was a small place. I was sure that whoever answered would be willing to direct me to a roadside assistance service.

It was a sensible, well-thought-out plan. Except for the part where I couldn't get the call to connect. That was the trouble with the modern world. Technology made us dependent on the bells and whistles. When they didn't work, we were up a creek.

Though my nose was cold and my eyes watered, I focused on plan B. Surely there was a home nearby. There were supposedly almost ten thousand inhabitants on this island, a quarter of whom lived in the largest town...Portree. That left 7500 souls to come to my assistance.

Though I wasn't as dedicated as Hayley when it came to researching our trip, I did know that I was in the midst of six hundred fifty square miles (give or take) of island territory, not all of which was connected by road. The population density was 6.04 people per square kilometer.

Even adjusting for the folks who lived in towns, surely there were at least a couple of people in shouting distance. I cupped my hands around my mouth. "Hellooo-ooo," I yelled.

The wavering sound disappeared, swallowed up by low clouds and the empty countryside. I fancied I saw a tiny light far in the distance, but my perspective was skewed. I sure as heck wasn't about to go striding across the moors in search of something that might not even be human habitation.

"Hellooo-ooo," I tried again, feeling foolish. Wasn't that the accepted definition of insanity? Doing the same thing over and over but expecting a different outcome?

It seemed I had two choices. I could start walking back to Portree. Or I could sit and wait for help that might never come. I wasn't really a sit-and-wait kind of gal, but I was wearing heels, and my comfy walking shoes were trapped in the trunk inside my suitcase.

Still, any activity was better than nothing...right?

I leaned against the car and took off one of my shoes. They were Manolo Blahniks. Wickedly expensive. Surprisingly comfortable. Currently useless. I balanced on one foot and used both hands to try and snap the heel from the base of the shoe. Turns out, old Manolo made a quality product. And he had an inside track on some kind of space glue, because no matter how hard I tried, I couldn't break the heel.

This struck me as ridiculously funny. I started to laugh and couldn't stop. Here I was, stranded in the middle of a seemingly unpopulated wilderness, hopping on one leg like an injured flamingo.

Suddenly, I flashed back to my childhood. One of my early nannies—when I was in kindergarten maybe—was a Cuban woman named Josefina Ortiz. She and her family had fled Cuba in the 1950s. Jo-Jo, as I called her, had a crush on Desi Arnaz, and she also liked to nap after lunch. She would sit me on the sofa beside her and tune the TV to a channel that showed old episodes of *I Love Lucy.*

With my little tummy full of homemade macaroni and cheese or gooey quesadillas, I leaned up against the solid, warm bulk of my nanny and listened to her snore softly while Lucy and Ethel got into one scrape after another.

In those moments I was safe and warm and loved.

The memory caught me off guard, bittersweet and faintly disturbing. I knew that my parents loved me, despite their foibles. I'd been brought up with every possible advantage and opportunity. Still, when I thought about my youngest years, the happiest memories were those I spent with women who were no blood kin to me at all.

Perhaps that was why I clung so stubbornly to my friendships with Hayley and Willow.

As I stood there, stork-like, caught in the past, a flash of bright light cut through the mist. Accompanying that herald was the muted roar of a vehicle. *Hallelujah.*

When the motorcycle pulled up beside my disabled car, I was too relieved to have any qualms about my safety. Besides, major crime was virtually non-existent in a place like this. I should know. I checked. When I decided to rent an isolated house for an entire month, it only made sense to weigh the pros and cons.

I put my shoe back on and wrapped my arms around my waist. A combination of the weather and the late hour made me shiver. "Hello," I said.

The driver cut the engine. Now the silence was twice as deep. He swung a leg over the seat, stretched, and removed his helmet. "Trouble, lass?"

"Not at all. I like tipping cars into ditches. It's something we do back home when there aren't any cows available."

The man froze, his hands caught mid-motion scraping back his wavy, jet-black hair. At least, I *thought* it was black. In the darkness it was hard to tell. I could just make out wide shoulders, a strong jaw, and the fact that he was more or less my age. Even in the dark, his masculinity and rugged good looks registered.

When he moved three steps closer, the back of my neck tingled. I'd always had a smart mouth. Some people didn't appreciate sarcasm.

"American, aren't you?"

Was that resignation I heard in his voice? "Yes, though I'm not sure what that has to do with my car being in a ditch."

The stranger shrugged. "Wrong side of the road. Happens all the time."

His unspoken criticism made me bristle. "I've traveled across six of the seven continents. This isn't my first rodeo. The only reason my car is in the ditch is because I swerved to keep from hitting an animal. So I would appreciate your removing that smirk." He didn't need to know that most of my travel had been done in groups…or that I rarely drove myself.

"My apologies, Duchess. Carry on."

Duchess? What did that mean? It sounded like sarcasm, but he didn't even know me. I watched, incredulous, as he turned back toward his motorcycle and picked up his helmet. Dressed in black leather from head to toe, tall, slim-hipped, and probably bad to the bone, he exuded disgust.

Then again, did his personality really matter in this situation?

"Wait," I cried. "I need help."

Chapter 4

Reluctance oozed from his posture. I'd pissed off my one and only rescuer. *Way to go, McKenzie.*

Summoning a conciliatory tone, I managed a smile. Though I was exhausted and cold and depressed because my trip was off to such a dismal start, I wasn't about to let this sharp-edged stranger witness my weakness. "I'm renting a cottage for the month. It must be nearby. According to my directions, I'm on the right route."

"I should hope so. There's only one main road here on the east side. Which cottage? What's the family's name?"

"I corresponded with a Mr. Cedric McCracken. He sent a key. I picked it up at the post office in Inverness." I reached in my pocket and extracted the small item as if physical proof would bolster my case. "See." I held out my hand.

"Hmph..."

The utterly masculine response worried me. There seemed to be a lot he wasn't saying. "Could you possibly take me there?" I asked, casting my pride to the wind. I believed a woman could and should be self-sufficient. This was a time to be realistic.

"Aye. I'll take you. At least you're wearing pants. 'Twill make the trip easier."

The pants to which he referred so dismissively were Chanel and matched my jacket. "Thank you very much," I replied, my tone grateful. "What should I do about my luggage?"

"If it's just the one suitcase, I'll come back for it and tie it to the rear of the bike. That will do for a short trip."

"Um..."

"What?"

I sensed his irritation. Perhaps he was miffed at being kept out in the chilly weather when he could be home by the fire. "Three cases in the trunk," I said. "Plus, my purse and carry-on. I can hold those two," I said quickly. I wanted him to know I was a team player.

"Three?" The word sounded strangled. As if he were trying not to laugh.

"I'm staying for a month. I like my creature comforts." It wasn't as if I could pop over to the nearest Duane Reade for personal items.

"You'll have to figure out the suitcases on your own tomorrow," he said bluntly. "I can tie the small bag behind us if you have your purse on your shoulder. You'll need to hang onto me. The road up to the McCracken house is in bad shape."

"You know it?" That seemed like a good sign. At least I hadn't rented a non-existent building from some scam artist.

He nodded. "I've been in it a time or two. Not for a year or more, though. Let's go."

Again, the impatience. Just my luck. The first interesting man I'd met in Scotland showed no inclination to shower me with attention and devotion. Where was a Jamie Fraser when you needed one?

"Of course," I said meekly. I wasn't about to ruffle this man's feathers. Though they were particularly gorgeous feathers, I'd be willing to bet that beneath all that supple black leather he wasn't soft at all.

I was prepared to fish for my belongings in the upended car. Before I could do it, my dark knight in shining armor hitched himself up and delved for what I needed. Where I had been clumsy and panting exiting the car, my mystery man made the whole exercise seem effortless.

He handed me my purse without speaking and turned to fasten my carry-on above the back fender of the motorcycle. "That should do it," he said. "Climb on. I don't have a passenger helmet, but we're not going far."

"Wait," I said. "I don't even know your name."

He fastened his chinstrap and slung a leg across the huge Harley. I knew zip about motorcycles, but I could read the logo easily enough.

When he was ready—and me still standing nearby metaphorically wringing my hands—he shot me a look. "Finley Craig. Now get on the damn bike."

"Yes, sir." Disgruntled, I put the strap of my purse crosswise over my chest. I didn't want to risk dropping it. Gingerly, I mounted behind Finley, found the spots to rest my feet, and encircled his waist with my arms.

Oh, my. He was a furnace, warming my chilled limbs and making me want to burrow against his back. Instead, I did just the opposite. I kept my spine straight and any cuddling tendencies to myself.

My hands at his waist had a death grip on his leather jacket.

"Hold on," he said. He fired the powerful engine, and we were off.

What happened next was difficult to describe. In some ways, it was like the wrenching sensation Claire Randall described when she stepped through a stone circle and vanished back in time. The world spun dizzily. With my eyes closed, I clung to my rescuer. The whole spine-straight thing was impractical at best. I rested my cheek against Finley's back.

All around me, the night was dark, the occasional lights in the distance no more than the blip of lightning bugs on a summer evening. Overhead, the twinkling stars blurred. Perhaps the planets halted in their orbits. Anything was possible.

I have no idea how long the trip lasted. Fifteen minutes? Twenty?

When we left the main road and turned up a narrow track, the motorcycle faltered momentarily. I heard Finley curse beneath his breath, the sound carried away on the night breeze.

"What's wrong?" I asked drowsily. If I had my way, we would have stayed out for hours riding the roads and absorbing the poetry of a wild Scottish night.

"Potholes," he said succinctly. "Ye'd best hold on tight. I'd not want to lose you."

I grinned, my amusement hidden behind his back. Those were the most romantic words any man had ever said to me. Accompanied by the frustration and disgust in Finley's deep voice, no woman could possibly get the wrong idea. My rescuer was more of an anti-hero. Reluctant, at best.

He wasn't kidding about the road. Despite Finley's care, the steep, unpaved track was getting the best of him. Every time Finley picked up speed, another pothole threatened to send us tumbling.

At last we reached our destination. The low, thatched-roof cottage sat desolate. No welcoming lights. No curl of smoke from the chimney.

I bit my lip hard, hoping the sharp pain would keep me from bawling. "I suppose they forgot I was coming today. Maybe someone had the date wrong."

"Hmpf." Again the word that wasn't a word, and yet communicated so much. He held my hand to steady me as I hopped off the bike. Then he followed suit. "Give me the key," he said.

I wanted to snap at him sarcastically. Something about bossiness and arrogance. At this juncture, I dared not alienate the only Good Samaritan who had come my way.

When Finley fit the key in the lock, it turned immediately. I exhaled. I'd been holding my breath unconsciously. Following him inside, I bumped up against him when he stopped suddenly and muttered.

"What?" I cried in alarm. "What is it?

"The power's not working. I imagine the old man forgot to pay the bill." As I absorbed that unpleasant thought, Finley located a flashlight on a shelf beside the front door. The narrow beam of light brought a sigh of relief…right up until the moment I fully absorbed the state of my getaway cabin.

Everything was covered in a thick layer of dust. A container of half-eaten donuts sat on the kitchen table. The mouse droppings around the package were hard to miss.

Swallowing a shudder, I followed Finley as he stepped gingerly around a pile of broken glass. The layout was simple. One large room contained the kitchen and living area. Beyond that were two small bedrooms with a connecting bath. The beds in each room were neatly made, but when I put my hand on the coverlets, the fabric was damp.

"Well," I said, my throat tight, "this isn't quite what I expected."

"The old man's been forgetful of late. He must have gone downhill fast. He has a daughter living in Glasgow. I imagine she fetched him to look after him...at least that's what I've heard. I'm sure she had no clue old Cedric had booked visitors."

"Only one. Just me." And now here I was, stuck in the middle of a dark night in a dwelling that might as well have come straight out of a horror movie. "No worries," I said breezily. "If you'll give me a lift back to town, I'll stay at one of the hotels and deal with all this in the morning."

We had returned to main living area. Finley stood, arms crossed, and stared at me. He trained the beam of the flashlight in my direction. "There's a music festival in town this weekend. Every hotel room is booked, plus all the B&Bs. You'd have to drive all the way back out to the mainland to find accommodations." He paused for what I could only assume was dramatic effect. "And you don't have a car."

The man was only stating the obvious. He could have said it with a bit more sympathy. The taciturn, grumpy biker hadn't even bothered to ask *my* name. Perhaps he thought there was no need, since he wouldn't be hanging around.

"Forgive me for asking," I said, my tone syrupy sweet. "Do you have a suggestion for what I might do? I'm tired and hungry and disappointed and all out of answers." I hadn't meant to be quite so honest. The words tumbled out uncensored.

Perhaps my unwitting vulnerability tapped into some latent chivalry on Finley's part. For the first time, his posture relaxed. "I do. My house is large. It's near the harbor, so you can walk most places. I'm listed in the B&B registry, though to be honest, I haven't said yes to any guests for a long time. Playing host is a lot of trouble. Still, ye're welcome to stay with me until you can make arrangements to have this place cleaned."

"Stay with you?" I parroted the words, my heart beating rapidly. Finley might not be the Loch Ness monster, but he was definitely an unknown quantity.

When I hesitated, he rubbed two fingers in the center of his forehead as if he had a headache. "I'm an upstanding citizen, more or less. As soon as we get back to town, you can look up the website. If you want to call the bloke who owns the seafood place down by the wharf, he'll vouch for me."

"I was there this evening. I have the phone number on the receipt, but I haven't been able to get a decent cell phone signal."

Finley shrugged. "You've found it," he said. His quick grin startled me.

"Found what?"

"The proverbial rock and the hard place."

He was a hundred percent correct. No woman in her right mind would try to spend a night alone in this grimy, unprepossessing dwelling. But most women also wouldn't agree to stay with a man they'd just met. With no cell service, my only choices were to walk back to town or take a chance on Finley Craig.

I lifted my chin, hoping he didn't see my unease. "Would you answer a few questions for me?"

"For you, Duchess, sure. Fire away."

"Why do you call me Duchess?"

"It's a nickname, that's all."

Evasion pure and simple, but I moved on. "Are you married?"

"No."

"Any children?"

"No."

"Have you ever been convicted of a felony?"

Long silence. "No."

My ruse was nothing more than a stall tactic. Finley might be lying to me with a straight face. Even so, I had to pretend to myself that I wasn't about to do something utterly reckless. "How do you know all the B&Bs are full?"

He shrugged. "There are a limited number of rooms to let on the island. You'd be surprised how often tourists make a spontaneous trip to Skye thinking they'll land wherever the wind blows them. Unfortunately, those same wanderers often find themselves out in the cold. Literally."

I knew he was telling the truth about that. A friend of mine had warned me not to take lodging for granted. At her admonition, I had made sure to have all my plans in place before I ever left home. Unfortunately, the confirmation letter in my purse was little comfort in this situation.

"Very well," I said, my stomach doing odd flips. "I appreciate your kind invitation. Yes. I'll stay with you tonight."

Chapter 5

I found it difficult to read Finley's emotions. Particularly when he was the one holding the flashlight. I frowned. "Have you changed your mind already?" He'd been silent for a good thirty seconds.

"Not at all. I was merely pausing to admire the fact that you aren't having hysterics about this crimp in your vacation."

I fought the urge to smack him. With my luck, I'd probably miss and throw out my shoulder. "First of all, this isn't a traditional vacation so much as it is a change of venue for me. I want to feel at home here…as if I belong. When I travel, I enjoy immersing myself in the local culture."

"I see."

"Second of all…" I took a deep breath, perilously close to doing exactly what he said. A nice, big hissy fit would feel good right about now. Nevertheless, I held onto my composure. "Your lame compliment is demeaning to me and to women in general. Most of us are quite capable of dealing with unforeseen circumstances. Women are neither weak nor helpless. I'm grateful for your help, yes. Still, in a pinch, I could have managed fine on my own."

Oh, wow, McKenzie. Why not tell another big whopper and get struck down by lightning?

"Duly noted, Duchess." Fortunately, he didn't call me on my B.S., though the dry note in his voice told me he saw through my bravado.

Without further ado, he scooted me out the door and locked it. Then he handed me the key. It was warm from his hand. I wrapped my fingers around it, clutching the bit of metal until the edges dug into my palm.

Earlier, when we arrived at the cottage, Finley had hooked his helmet around one handlebar of the bike. Now he picked it up and handed it to me. "Put this on."

"It will give me hat hair," I protested.

"Better than smashed skull hair."

I sensed that he wouldn't be moved on this issue. Reluctantly, I eased the helmet over my head. It felt claustrophobic. I tucked the strands of my platinum blond, shoulder-length bob inside. In a few years, I would probably need help from a bottle. For now, the color was all mine.

"Satisfied?" I asked.

"That remains to be seen, Duchess."

Whoa. Even in the dark, I couldn't miss the innuendo. I had a feeling the man didn't even like me. Suddenly, sexual tension swirled in the misty air around us. "I have a name," I said. "McKenzie Taylor."

He shrugged. "I like Duchess better. It suits you."

"You don't even know me."

He held out his hand. "Give me your purse," he said. "It's too far back to town for you to hold it."

Before I could protest, he lifted the tote over my head, secured the zipper, and wadded it up to fit beneath the bungee cords he had used to tether my carry-on. Though I winced at his careless handling of my big turquoise bag, he was right. It was miles back to town, and I would have been very uncomfortable.

"What about you?" I protested. "*You* don't have a helmet. I don't want to be responsible for you if we crash."

His quick grin was a flash of white in the gloom. "I'm hardheaded as they come," he said. "Ask anyone." He mounted the bike and held out a hand to steady me as I performed the same maneuver.

Instinctively, I slid my arms around his taut waist and nestled as close as I could. The provocative position gave me all sorts of ideas. I'd never been on a "hog" before.

When the engine roared to life, I jumped and nearly fell off. Finley tried to turn his laugh into a cough. I wasn't fooled. My cheeks flaming, I settled into my assigned spot, glad he couldn't actually see me.

What was he thinking as we made our way back down the drive? A man with his looks probably spent many a day or night riding the roads with an available woman at his back. Maybe he barely even noticed me clinging to him like a limpet.

Once we turned out onto the main road where the pavement was reliable, I relaxed a bit. Finley was not a novice. Unlike me, he was extremely comfortable on his bike. He wasn't going to dump us in a ditch.

It was impossible to talk as we sped along. That was fine by me. I had a lot to think about. I'd fantasized about this Scotland trip so many times that Willow was probably right. I'd set myself up for disappointment.

On the other hand, I had already been rescued by a handsome Scotsman, so maybe my fantasy life and my love life were finally going to align, along with the stars. Now if only I could find someone a bit less grumpy and a bit more polished. Frankly, I'd never been drawn to the bad-boy type, though I could try to make an exception in Finley's case.

To be fair, I shouldn't peg the man without giving him a chance. He might be an architect or a banker. I snickered, my cheek mashed against the warm leather on his back. Not likely. He exuded a raw sex appeal more suited to rock 'n' roll or dark poetry or maybe even larceny.

Two hundred years ago these islands had sheltered many a smuggler, some benign…others more vicious. Even now in the twenty-first century, bad men still walked among us. Still, my gut told me Finley Craig was a stand-up kind of guy. I had to believe that, or why else was I blithely letting him take me back to his lair?

I was cold and tired and basically homeless, but I couldn't feel too upset about my misfortunes. This evening was the most excitement I'd had in my life for far too long. I'd been a model daughter…a model citizen for that matter. People respected me and relied on me. My friends, even the ones who didn't go as far back in my history as Hayley and Willow, knew they could count on me in a crisis. Never once had I done anything truly reckless.

Now here I was, doubling on a wicked Harley-Davidson with Temptation himself. Already I could imagine the two of us taking long walks on a storm-washed beach. Or listening to classical music in a cozy room while I edited my photographs and Finley smoked a pipe. The image made me chuckle. Willow and I thought Hayley was naïve, but I was something far more dangerous. I was a dream weaver. A teller of tales.

Rarely did I allow anyone to see that side of me. Not even my two best friends. My imagination had kept me company during long years as an only child. Whenever I was sad that my parents weren't around, I invented cousins and exotic aunts and uncles who whisked me away for weekends in Paris. Or long summer vacations at a cottage on the coast.

Without warning, Finley braked and put his feet on the ground, keeping us upright. I think I was practically asleep when the motorcycle crested a hill and we looked down on the lights of Portree. The small town sat like an elongated bowl, sweeping down to the harbor. From our vantage point, I could see the waterfront and the line of businesses and restaurants where I had eaten dinner earlier. The facades were painted in colorful shades reminiscent of Rainbow Row in Charleston, South Carolina.

I wondered if Finley was planning to make good on his assertion that a fellow townsman could vouch for him. We wound down the hill at a sedate speed. Finley parked the bike and helped me off. I handed over the helmet and fussed with my hair. He insisted no one would bother my carry-on, but I wanted my tote.

When he held my elbow as we walked down a flight of stone stairs, I didn't fuss. A broken ankle would be no way to start my adventure. Soon we were standing in front of a familiar building.

"They're closed," I said, pointing at the sign in the window.

"He'll still be here cleaning up and doing prep for tomorrow." Finley used his fist to drum a tattoo on the glass. Moments later, a man I recognized peeked out from a hallway at the back of the room and hurried to open the door for us.

Finley ushered me inside. "McKenzie, this chap is Hamish Doune. We've know each other for a decade. Tell her, Hamish. Tell her I have a respectable room to rent. Tell her I'm not a threat."

The restaurateur was a giant of a man with big hands that, incongruously, held a bleached muslin dishcloth. He dried his fingers slowly, his gaze darting from Finley to me and back again. "A threat?"

I perched on a barstool. My legs were quivery. It had been a long day with no prospect of bed anytime soon. "I've rented Cedric McCracken's house for the month. When I arrived, the place was a mess. Apparently, he forgot I was coming."

Hamish winced. "Aye…the dementia. He's gone to Glasgow, I heard. With his daughter."

Finley had been right. Portree was a small town with no secrets. I nodded. "The cottage is actually unlivable at the moment. I'm sure I can find a heavy cleaning service…can't I? Mr. Craig has offered to let me stay with him until the house is fit to be occupied."

Without asking, Hamish poured three shots of whiskey and passed one to me before handing Finley a small glass. "*Sláinte*!"

Finley leaned against the bar. Hamish lounged in the doorway that led to the back. In unison, the two men tilted their heads and knocked back the liquor with a shudder and a sigh of appreciation.

I stared at the small serving of amber liquid. On many occasions I had ordered fancy cocktails in flawless French. In Paris. And not to boast, but I was somewhat of a wine connoisseur when it came to Italian vintages. I confess, though, that I had never particularly enjoyed hard spirits.

Hamish grinned, noting my ambivalence. "Try it, lass. There's none like it for miles. This is my private stash. For VIPs only."

Finley only smiled, raising my temperature and making me dizzy.

With the two men staring at me, I could either plead abstinence or be rude or drink the damn stuff. With a quick prayer for luck, I downed the whiskey and thumped the glass on the bar.

For a few seconds, nothing happened. Then a nuclear warhead went off in my stomach. It had been several hours since dinner, so my belly was empty. Hamish's whiskey was potent stuff. My eyes watered. My face turned red. I felt a little queasy.

"Very nice," I said primly.

Both men roared with laughter. I merely held out my glass and said, "One more for the road?"

Hamish blinked. Finley glared. "Don't you dare. I'm not carrying you up to the guest room."

Even Hamish turned red this time. He frowned at Finley. "Don't go propositioning the lass. She's a visitor to our fair isle. We must treat her with care and respect."

Hamish looked at me, his expression cajoling. "Forgive him, lass. He has a bit of the devil in him, but there's no finer man on Skye. Finley doesn't take in tourists on a regular basis, but if he's offered you a room for a few nights, it's an invitation with no strings attached. I'll stake my reputation on it."

Chapter 6

Most of my reservations melted away. "Thank you, Mr. Doune," I said. That means a lot." I turned back to Finley who once again leaned indolently against the bar. "I'd kill for a bed," I said, being entirely honest. "May we go now?"

Finley straightened slowly. Here in Hamish's restaurant, I was seeing my rescuer properly for the first time. His broad forehead, classically handsome nose, and strong jaw created a face that was stunning masculine and completely unforgettable.

I think his eyes were my weak spot. Coal-black lashes framed blue irises the shade of pure sapphires. A woman could be hypnotized by those eyes if she weren't on her guard.

Perhaps he was fair-skinned at birth, but he had clearly spent a lot of time in the sun, as his skin was golden brown. Around those remarkable eyes were tiny white crinkle lines, which told me not only was he outdoors a lot, but that he laughed. Often. Somehow, I found that hard to believe. With me, Finley Craig had been intense and moody and more like judge and jury than friend.

His hair was thick and shiny black, like a raven's wing. It was too long to be short, but not long enough to make a statement. Like the man, his hair was an enigma.

Hamish took pity on me. "Ye sure you don't want one more drink? Jet lag can be a real pisser. You're dead on your feet, lass. Another shot will send you off to dreamland for sure."

I stood up carefully, feeling the unaccustomed alcohol swirl in my stomach. "Thank you for the drink, Mr. Doune. But I'll pass. I didn't have the chance to tell you earlier. The seafood this evening was amazing."

"I thought I recognized you. Ye had the table in the corner, right? And Lara waited on you?"

"Right on both counts. How do you remember all that?"

"It's my restaurant…my livelihood. I make it my business to take note of who comes and goes. Ye'd be surprised at who drops in now and again thanks to our Finley."

"Hamish…"

I sensed a clear note of warning in Finley's voice, though I had no idea why. "It was lovely to meet you," I said, shaking the big man's hand. Then I turned to Finley. "I'm exhausted. Do you mind if we go?"

He shook his head. "Not at all. This stop was for your peace of mind."

The two men thumped each other on the back in a quick semblance of a hug—the way men do—and then we were on our way.

It was all I could do to make it back up the steps to where the motorcycle was parked. If I hadn't lingered in Inverness, if I had driven straight to Skye, I would have found out about the cottage many hours before now and might possibly even have snagged the last of the available rooms at the hotel.

If ifs and buts were candy and nuts…

It was too late now. My adventure was starting out inauspiciously, but things would look better in the morning. Fortunately, Finley's house was not far away.

We cut through an alleyway onto a narrow road that accessed the hill behind the restaurant. The view overlooking the water would be spectacular in the daylight, but it was well and truly dark by now. Nestled in a small copse of trees sat a house that looked as if it had emerged straight out of a fairytale.

Perhaps at one time it had been two separate dwellings. The current home crept up the hill as if the builder had not known where to stop. The old whitewashed structure had glass panes that were off kilter and window boxes filled with pansies.

I fell in love with it on sight.

Finley gave me no time to linger. He ushered me inside and immediately went to light the small pile of wood and kindling that had already been laid in the hearth. Soon, the fire flickered and popped, giving off an unmistakable scent that took me back to winter evenings in Switzerland.

My parents would never have tolerated anything so messy as real burning logs, even if such a thing had been practical in Atlanta or Manhattan. But on ski trips, I remember sitting around the fire and drowsily listening to the grownups talk about the day's runs.

"Are you hungry?"

Finley's words startled me. I'd been lost in thought, far away from this small Scottish gem of a town.

I nodded. "I could eat. Nothing much. Maybe some milk to offset that whiskey."

He led me through a narrow hallway into a kitchen that looked as if it belonged in one of the dormitories at Hogwarts. Finley put a hand on my shoulder. "Sit."

While he prepared our snack of popcorn and hot chocolate, I rested my head on my arms. The surface of the rough-hewn table was hard but smooth, as if generations of schoolchildren had breakfasted in this very same spot.

I managed to eat half of my popcorn and drink all of the warm beverage. My eyes were so heavy I could barely hold them open.

Finley took pity on me. "I'll save the tour for the morning," he said. "Let's get you to bed before you fall over."

I wanted to make a snappy comeback to throw him off his stride. I was rapidly discovering, however, that Finley was not easily rattled.

Suddenly, a thump against the door on the opposite side of the kitchen caught Finley's attention. He jumped up, turned the knob, and backed away as a good-sized blur of fur and energy burst into the room. The dog was a beauty, with long droopy ears and a playful disposition.

My exhaustion forgotten for the moment, I crouched by my chair and laughed out loud when the puppy launched itself in my direction and licked my face enthusiastically.

"Down, girl. Sit. Stay. Cinnamon!" Finley tried, but to no avail.

"Oh, she's a beauty," I said. "And she's not hurting anything…are you, love?" The animal recognized a kindred spirit and allowed me to cuddle her without protest. She even looked at Finley soulfully as if to say, *This lady gets me.*

"She's an English cocker. Her paws may be dirty," Finley warned. "She'll ruin your pants."

"Oh, pooh. They're only pants, aren't they, baby girl?" The dog was warm and affectionate, and I found myself with tears in my eyes for no other reason than that I was a little bit homesick. I kept my head down and my attention on the pup so Finley wouldn't see my distress.

By now, I should have been tucked inside my charming Scottish cottage with my belongings neatly put away in an antique bureau and a pot of hot tea on the stove. Instead, I was stranded in a stranger's house with nothing to look forward to tomorrow than the unexciting prospect of tracking down a cleaning crew and a tow-truck for the car.

Finley whistled. Cinnamon hung her head.

A second whistle, and the dog abandoned me.

"She stays in my office when I'm away or if I have company. Otherwise, she has the run of the house," Finley explained.

I sniffed and managed a watery smile. "Don't exile her on my account. I like animals. I was never allowed to have any growing up, and now my housekeeper has allergies, so I still don't have a dog or a cat. I'd love for Cinnamon to hang out with me as much as she wants."

Finley stared at me, his gaze narrowed. "I can't figure you out, Duchess."

"What do you mean?"

"Well, you travel with enough luggage for a visiting head of state, you don't mind if a dog ruins your couture clothes, and because of an employee's issues, you choose not to have a pet you desperately want."

"Hilda's not *just* an employee," I protested. "She's been with me for almost a decade. She was one of my babysitters when I was growing up. After I left for college, my mother kept her on as a maid, and once I returned to Atlanta and settled into my own place, Hilda came to work for me. Not having a pet is a small sacrifice, believe me. Hilda and I go way back."

"I see."

I wasn't sure that he did. What did it matter? Finley and I were ships that passed in the night. As soon as I had a working vehicle and a livable accommodation, I was out of here.

Without further cross-examination, my host led me out of the kitchen and up a narrow flight of stairs to the second floor. I could swear Finley's home didn't have a single right angle anywhere. The walls and floors and staircases moved drunkenly in all directions. However, the place was rock solid.

Too bad it didn't have some of the moving staircases from the Harry Potter books. No telling when one would come in handy in this house.

The guest quarters were reassuringly normal, at least the ones to which I was assigned. I surveyed the bed. It was generous for a single person, larger than the twins back home but not exactly a full size or a queen. The coverlet was made of heavy brown cotton embroidered with Celtic symbols in green and lavender.

On the hardwood floor, woolen rugs lay scattered here and there. The single window was shuttered for the night. Cinnamon nuzzled my leg with her head as if seeking a nod of approval.

"This is lovely," I said. "I do appreciate everything you've done for me. I'm sorry to be such a bother."

Finley shrugged, a small smile playing around the corners of his mouth. "No bother at all. We have a reputation to uphold here on the island. It wouldn't do for word to get out that old Cedric stranded a pretty American tourist and no one came to her rescue. I'll go get your bag off the back of the bike. Feel free to explore the facilities. I think you'll find everything you need."

While Finley was gone, Cinnamon and I made our way into the small but charming bathroom. The tank for the commode was high on a wall with a pull chain for flushing. A white, enameled cabinet hid towels, toothbrushes, and various other amenities. A tiny, blue glass vase on the sink held a single pansy. The place was spotless.

I doubted Finley was the kind of man to scrub floors, so he must have a housekeeper. Perhaps that person could direct me to someone who would be able to attack Cedric's house. "Well, Cinnamon," I said, "I guess you're stuck with me for a day or two."

Finley returned with my carry-on bag as I spoke to the dog. He grimaced. "Don't get your hopes up. I don't know which is the bigger challenge—getting your car out of the ditch or having someone tackle that house. Both problems will probably require patience."

"I can be patient," I said mildly. Staying with Finley wasn't exactly a hardship. I didn't want to be a burden. "And perhaps if I can get the car fixed, I should simply clean the house myself. It's not all that big."

"Don't be daft," he said, the grimace turning into a frown. "You've no supplies or equipment. It would take you days. And besides, do you really want to spend your vacation on your hands and knees?"

My eyes widened. I blinked and swallowed. Finley went stock still as a tide of red rushed from his neck to his face when he realized what he had said.

He backpedaled quickly. "Cleaning the floors, I mean."

"I know what you meant." My muttered response did nothing to ease the awkwardness. We stood on either side of a soft, cozy bed. He was a man. I was a woman. To be painfully honest, it had been far too long since I had met anyone as fascinating as Finley Craig.

Cinnamon lay on the floor with her head on her paws, her gaze darting back and forth between her master and me. Dogs were sensitive creatures. Did she understand that all was not well?

Finley stared at me for the longest time. At least it seemed that way. Had his thoughts wandered down the same dangerous path? He nodded curtly. "I should go. You need your sleep. There's no rush in the morning. You'll find toast and fruit in the kitchen whenever you wake up."

"Thank you." I picked at the edge of the coverlet, wondering how many tourists he rescued each month and how many propositioned him in return. *Bad girl, bad McKenzie.*

"Is there anything else you need?"

I could think of quite a few answers to that question, but I settled for the most socially acceptable one. "My pajamas are in a suitcase in the trunk of my car. Do you have something I could wear to sleep in?"

Chapter 7

The red in his neck deepened. "Of course." He cleared his throat. "Give me just a moment. I won't bother you again. I'll hang a shirt on the doorknob. Goodnight, Duchess. Come on, Cinnamon."

"Oh, please let her stay. I'd enjoy her company."

I could swear the dog understood every word. Cinnamon rubbed against my legs, her tail wagging enthusiastically.

Finley hesitated. "I'll need to take her out soon."

"Can it wait until I've showered? I'd be happy to do the honors. I won't forget, I promise."

"If you're sure. You'll need to put her on a leash when you go out. The harness is on a nail beside the kitchen door. She's stronger than she looks. If she gets loose, I'll be half the night finding her."

"I'll be careful, I promise. Goodnight, Finley. Thank you again for everything."

When he left with only a brusque nod of his head and closed the door behind him, I sank into a chair and exhaled slowly. Cinnamon laid her head on my knee. Stroking the dog's ears absentmindedly, I wondered if I had the energy left to get in the shower. On the other hand, I'd been traveling all day and that bed was clean and sweet smelling. The sheets had been dried in the sun. It was hard to fake that scent.

Cinnamon made a perfect, undemanding companion. I talked to her as I washed my face and brushed my teeth. She guarded the bathroom door while I showered. Afterward, I thought the hairdryer might spook her, but she watched, rapt, as I used the small appliance and a round brush to put the sleek curve back in my hair.

With a towel wrapped around my damp body, I tiptoed across the bedroom. After pressing my ear to the door and hearing nothing, I opened it a crack and stuck out my hand to feel the knob. Finley had made good on his promise. He'd left me one of his shirts, a much-laundered, faded blue chambray that came down almost to my knees.

I rinsed out my bra and undies and left them hanging on a bar in the bathroom. They would be dry by morning. My only remaining problem was what to wear on my feet when I went outside to let Cinnamon do her business. Oh well, it wouldn't take long. And it was summer, after all. A Scottish summer, but summer nevertheless.

"Are you ready, girl?"

She scampered to the door, tail wagging madly.

Mindful of Finley's warning. I found the leash exactly as he had described it. Cinnamon was already wearing a collar, so it was a simple matter to fasten the braided length of mesh to a loop and check that it was tight.

Before I opened the door, I wrapped the leash around my hand so there would be no surprises. "Behave yourself," I muttered. "Do what you have to do and let's go back inside so I can sleep." There was no sign of Finley. Presumably his bedroom was on another level of the odd house.

Outside, the night was cool and fragrant. Though my feet were bare, the cobblestoned walkway wasn't difficult to negotiate. Cinnamon barked at a squirrel and chased a moth. Soon, she found a spot near a tree and took care of urgent needs.

Suddenly, I was in no real hurry to go back inside. Here I was, halfway around the globe from my life back in the States. My whole plan was a bust so far, but that was the nature of travel at times. I couldn't regret meeting Finley. His sweet, goofy dog was a bonus.

Emboldened by a sudden burst of energy, I stepped cautiously out into the road. As far as I could tell, Finley's was the only house up here. The lane ended in a cul-de-sac just beyond where I was standing. I curled my toes against the pavement. It still held a trace of warmth from the heat of the day.

"Oh, Cinnamon," I said. "How did I wind up in such a mess?" Even if I hadn't wrecked the car, I still would have been faced with the wretched condition of Cedric's rental house.

The dog pulled at the leash, eager to explore. I was warm and comfortable in the long-sleeved shirt, so I let her lead me down the hill a few steps. As we rounded a curve, I caught a glimpse of the harbor below. Lights on boat masts bobbed up and down like nautical fireflies. I wondered if Finley sailed. I'd had several friends over the years who were boat people. Though I loved the water, I'd never had any desire to learn the ins and outs of sailing. Perhaps this would be the time to try.

A huge yawn took me by surprise, popping my jaw. "Come on, girl. Time to go in."

She whined and sat down.

Good grief. Were we really going to have a battle of wills at this hour? "Please be a good puppy. Let's get back to the house. I saw your water bowl in the kitchen. I'll bet there's a treat there, too."

Cinnamon was unimpressed. She cocked her head as if to point out the stars and convince me this was the best time of day to play. A single, happy bark emphasized her point.

"I get it," I said, smiling even though my legs felt like spaghetti and my whole body ached. "It's a gorgeous evening." In Scotland, no less. Suddenly, I flashed to a vision of Jamie Fraser galloping over the hill on horseback, ready to scoop me up and put me behind him as we rode off into the wild night.

Hayley and Willow and I had promised to look for our own versions of *Outlander*'s hero, Jamie Fraser, while we were in Scotland. Unfortunately, I didn't think Finley was mine. He did have the same striking face as my TV crush, though the eye color and shade of hair were all wrong. Even worse, the timing was off kilter.

Everyone knew that in a TV drama the lead can't work out all the details of the plot until the last five minutes. Fate certainly wasn't going to hand me Prince Charming with so little fanfare. Any prize worth having deserved a quest…a hunt…an adventure. I was going to be here for almost an entire month. I'd likely have to sort through a handful of candidates at least before I found my one true love.

I giggled, a little high on sleep deprivation and my near-nakedness. Besides, there was something about Finley, something not quite right. I couldn't put my finger on it, but it made me skittish.

He was gorgeous, yes. His in-your-face masculinity gave off a sexual vibe that made my breath catch and my heart beat faster. A man like Finley wouldn't be easy to control. Sadly, I crossed him off my mental list. I was a woman who *always* liked being in control. Whether it was in the bedroom or the boardroom, I wanted to call the shots.

Too bad Finley Craig wasn't the amenable type. Because he definitely revved my engines.

Cinnamon went still, her hair standing on end. She growled low in her throat. Suddenly, a rodent of some sort darted out of the brush and scampered right in front of the dog's nose.

The puppy went wild, almost wrenching my arm from its socket as she bounded after the tiny mammal. I hung on to the leash for dear life, wincing as my feet trod on tiny twigs and stones. "Enough!" I cried. "Stop!"

My commands fell on deaf ears. The dog was in full-on attack mode. She ran and ran, zigzagging back and forth between trees, making no real progress. At last she darted into the narrow road again. I knew this was my chance. I planted my bare feet, held the leash with two hands, and yelled, "Cinnamon. Enough."

Unfortunately, my urgency got through. The puppy stopped dead in her tracks for a split second. I took a step forward. "Good girl. Let's—"

Before I could corral her, she was off again. The unexpected movement caught me off guard. I stumbled and went down hard on both knees. "Ouch, you wretched dog. Stop this instant."

At last she understood and acknowledged me. Circling back to where I sat in the road, she nosed my elbow and whined.

I scowled. "See what you made me do?"

Cinnamon groveled, penitent and pitiful.

My knees stung like the devil. Though it was dark, I was positive I had left a layer of skin on the pavement. When I touched my kneecap delicately, it was wet. *Great. Just great.*

Carefully, moving like an old lady, I got to my feet, wincing with every movement. I tugged on the leash. "Home, you rascal. Maybe we'll come out again tomorrow night," I said. "For now I'm done. Seriously. Play time is over."

Our pace was almost sedate as we made our way back to the house. Once we were inside the kitchen, I had my first clear look at my injuries. My knees were a raw, bloody mess. If I were at home, this situation would call for hydrogen peroxide. I was in a stranger's house, though, and I had no idea whether or not the Scots even used such a thing.

Cinnamon was suspiciously docile as I unfastened her leash and returned it to its allotted location. I put a finger to my lips. "Quiet," I whispered. "We don't want to wake the master of the house."

Despite our tiptoeing about, the stairs were old and creaked accordingly. I had no idea what time it was, but it was late. We had almost made it to the safety of my room when Finley appeared from around a corner, scowling. "Where in the hell have you been, Duchess? I thought you'd absconded with my dog."

It was clearly a joke. His tone annoyed me. "I'm sorry we woke you. I didn't know there was a time limit on these things. It's a beautiful night."

"I thought you were tired."

"I was. I *am*. Cinnamon wanted to play."

"She always does." He held out a hand. "I think she'd better sleep in my study. Puppies need a firm hand to learn discipline."

"Puppies also need love," I reminded him, indignant on Cinnamon's behalf. My knees hurt, but I wasn't going to whine about that.

"This mutt is a pro at getting what she wants, aren't you, girl?"

As if sensing what side her bread was buttered on, Cinnamon betrayed me and went to her master. Rubbing her head against his leg, she gave me a soulful look as if to apologize for her defection. "Fine," I muttered. "Good night."

I had my hand on the bedroom door when Finley barked out another order. "Stop. Wait." The man could give lessons to a drill sergeant.

Before I could respond, he was crouched in front of me, his fingers on the backs of my legs. "You're hurt, Duchess."

I shrugged. "It's nothing."

He looked up at me. "I told you she liked to run away."

Cinnamon pleaded with me telepathically.

"It wasn't her fault," I said. "She took me by surprise."

"Uh, huh." Finley brushed his thumb across one raw knee.

"Ouch! That hurts."

"We've got to get this cleaned up. You don't want to ruin your trip with a bad infection."

Before I could divine his intent, he scooped me up in his arms, bumped the door open with his hip, and laid me on the bed. "Don't move," he said. "I'll get the first aid kit."

Chapter 8

Cinnamon rested her nose on the edge of the mattress, looking as penitent as a puppy could. I could swear she was asking forgiveness.

I scratched her head and grinned when her eyes closed in ecstasy. "You're so easy," I said. "Fickle, aren't you?"

Finley reappeared. "She is at that. Move, you big galumph." He sat down near my hip and began digging through his cache of supplies.

I jerked upright abruptly, tugging the shirt to my knees. "Does that mean me, or the dog?"

The man actually grinned. It didn't last long. I sensed that it was reluctant humor at best, but I felt a sense of accomplishment.

"Very funny, Duchess. Hold still while I do this. You've got bits of dirt and debris mixed in with the blood."

After that, I couldn't think of a thing to say, comic or otherwise. Finley Craig handled my legs with all the dispassion of a medical professional. From where I was sitting, it felt extremely personal.

First, he tucked a towel beneath my thighs to protect the bedding. Then, without any warning at all, he dumped half a bottle of hydrogen peroxide over one kneecap and then the other. I shuddered and winced. The sting and the burn weren't pleasant, though the white fizziness did give me some reassurance that the liquid was doing its job.

Next, my amateur physician patted my knees dry with a paper towel and gently spread a thin film of antibiotic cream over the large expanses of scraped skin. He was careful…almost tender. When I sneaked a peek at his face, I noted his frown.

"I'm sorry to be such a bother," I said meekly. "I could have managed on my own."

"With what?" Finley head snapped up. His eyes flashed as he called me out on my bravado. I didn't like having to rely on anyone else, but in this case, he was right.

"Does it need a bandage?" I asked.

"Don't be so impatient. I'm about to cover it for the night so the medicine stays in place."

"Yes, sir." I nearly snapped a salute. The hour was late and my judgment was impaired, so I squashed the impulse.

Finley ignored my smart-ass response as he fastened a square adhesive bandage across each knee. "You can leave these off during the day tomorrow if you want to…or wait until the day after." He finished his task and straightened. His handiwork wasn't my most fashionable look, but my legs weren't aching as much.

He picked up the first aid kit. "Come on, Cinnamon. It's a night in the office for you, my girl."

This time I let it slide. I wasn't a pro when it came to canine training, but I had to admit I hated watching the sweet, rambunctious dog trot out the door. "Thank you, Finley," I said. "I'm sorry I let her get away from me."

He turned, his hand on the doorframe. "You're welcome." He paused and rubbed his chin. "Be honest, Duchess. Are you wearing anything at all under my shirt?"

I felt my face go hot. "No," I said. "I'm not."

* * * * * * *

I think I must have dozed off the moment the door closed behind my host and his dog. I slept deeply. When I awoke hours later, I felt reasonably rested and refreshed for the first time since leaving the States a few days ago. The problems that had seemed overwhelming last night were more like inconveniences this morning.

But first, breakfast…

After dressing in the same white pantsuit and silk tank, I padded barefoot down to the kitchen. Though I was accustomed to getting my caffeine fix via tea while in the UK, Finley owned an honest-to-god coffee pot. And it was almost full. Hallelujah! I inhaled the aroma like a junkie anticipating a fix.

In one of the cabinets, I found a collection of mismatched mugs. I chose the one that said *Bikers Do It On the Run.* I wasn't exactly sure what to make of that slogan, but the heavy ceramic cup was the biggest of the lot, and I needed a jolt of java to get me through this day.

Cinnamon was nowhere to be seen or heard. Perhaps she was with her master, out for a morning run, or more likely, off at work. Come to think of it, what exactly did Finley do for a living?

I sat at the round oak table, chin propped on one hand, and drank my coffee slowly, willing it to perk me up. Finley had left the toaster and a loaf of bread in a prominent position on the counter, but I wasn't hungry.

I was halfway through my second cup when I heard the front door open. Moments later, man and dog appeared. Cinnamon must have taken Finley's scolding to heart, because instead of bounding across the room, she went to the corner where her water dish sat, slurped up a mouthful, and curled up to study the humans.

"You make good coffee." I lifted my mug in greeting. To the man, not the dog.

Finley nodded. "I had a feeling you were a coffee woman."

"I might have a wee Starbucks addiction," I admitted.

"How are your knees?"

I nearly choked on a sip of hot coffee. "Better." Scintillating conversation. Wow.

He tossed a slip of paper on the table. "I spoke to woman I know in the village. She and her daughter promised to clean your house tomorrow. That was the soonest I could find anyone who was free. There's the phone number. Her name is Mrs. Clark. I told her you'd meet her at Cedric's place at nine in the morning."

My mouth hung open. "Excuse me?"

He shrugged. "You were asleep. I know the people here. It seemed like the most efficient way to proceed."

I tamped down my temper with an effort. The man was trying to help. "I'm accustomed to taking care of my own business," I said, "though it's kind of you to make those arrangements on my behalf." The words I spoke aloud were certainly much nicer than what I really wanted to say.

Finley continued, unfazed by my oblique reprimand. "The car rental place in Inverness will be out with a replacement vehicle and a truck to do the tow before dark tonight. They'll likely be able to force the trunk open so you can get your things. You'll have to sign some paperwork. It shouldn't be a problem."

I cocked my head. "Were you ever in the military?"

His eyes widened. "God, no. Do I look like the kind of guy who does well with authority?"

He had me there. What he looked like was a fallen angel. "I don't mean to sound ungrateful, but from now on, I'd prefer to handle my own arrangements. I'm sure you're a busy man."

"In other words, keep your arse out of my business, Mr. Craig."

"I didn't say that…exactly."

He chuckled. "You were thinking really loudly."

Wrinkling my nose, I stood and poured my third cup. "Don't take it personally." I had to pass far too close to him on the way to the coffeepot. He smelled like the soap from his shower and the freshness of a Highland morning. I told myself I wasn't impressed.

Striving for nonchalance, I leaned against the counter and eyed him over the rim of my biker mug. "Do you mind if I ask what you do for a living?"

He poured himself coffee as well, turned a chair around backward and straddled it. "I suppose not."

Stubborn man. "Well," I said, reining in my impatience. "Don't make me beg."

"That's one of my spe-cial-i-ties." He said it all British and proper. When he waggled his eyebrows, I had to laugh.

"Seriously, Finley. What do you do?"

He shrugged. "I build high-end motorcycles for individuals who can afford them."

"As in the rich and famous?"

"Aye. We normally start by sharing ideas via e-mail. I come up with sketches. When I get far enough along, the buyer comes to Skye for a firsthand look and a test drive. It's peaceful here…quiet. No paparazzi. No one to blink an eye if Jay Leno drops by for a modified Ducati with a Rolls Royce turbine engine."

"Jay Leno? Seriously?"

"He and Justin Timberlake, among others."

I studied his face for a long minute. "How does one get into that line of work?" I asked.

"That's a story for another day." The words were flat. Definitive. He finished his coffee and carried the cup to the sink. "I assume you can amuse yourself, lass. The town of Portree is at your disposal. I'd recommend lunch at the *Boar and Brigand.* My housekeeper will be by in a bit. She usually makes up a shepherd's pie for my dinner. If that suits you, you're welcome to share."

"Aren't you going to show me your workshop?" Suddenly, the prospect of being on my own had lost its charm.

He hesitated, clearly trying to formulate a polite answer. "I'm in the middle of a few things. Maybe tomorrow."

I nodded, refusing to admit that my feelings were hurt. I had lots of friends who *wanted* to spend time with me. Finley's gruff, barely tolerant attitude was disconcerting. "Fine. I'll do some exploring today. If I'm not back by six, feel free to eat without me."

As a parting shot, I hoped it expressed my utter lack of interest in him and his activities. I might be on the lookout for a Scotsman like Jamie Fraser, but I wasn't going to settle for a poor imitation. Never mind that in *Outlander*, Jamie was gruff and rude to Claire on more than one occasion. Only when she deserved it, though.

I put my host out of my mind and set off on foot to explore the small town of Portree. Finley was right about the lack of rooms. I checked at one hotel to make sure. The desk clerk's apologetic smile reinforced the truth. With the music festival in town, there was nary a bed to be had.

Would my cleaning ladies be able to finish Cedric's house in a single day? The place was in bad shape. Sadly, I wasn't at all confident that my host wouldn't toss me out on the street if it took too long for me to move on. He struck me as the kind of man who liked to spend time alone.

At the waterfront, I wandered aimlessly, strolling around the concrete wharf. With a small pair of binoculars I kept in my jacket pocket, I amused myself reading the names of the various boats docked in the harbor. *LadyBird, SeaLily, Pride of Portree.* Apart from Skye, there were dozens of islands west of where I stood, not all of them inhabited.

Unlike Skye, there were no bridges to access the Outer Hebrides. It was the car ferry or a puddle jumper. I'd been warned that the ferry was unreliable, not because of staff or vehicles, but in light of the changeable weather. Wind or rain could and did derail many a travel plan.

I wasn't too worried. I first wanted to spend at least a week at my rental house settling in and creating my nest. After that, I would make a point of exploring the entire island. Once those goals were ticked off the list, maybe I'd consider spending a few nights farther afield.

It was amusing, in a way, that on the Isle of Skye—where I felt a million miles away from home—there were still mysterious bits of Scotland even *more* remote. Places with names like Iona, Eigg, Mull, and Uist. The Gaelic language and the old religions still thrived in many of those places. Because of my fascination with all things Scottish, I think I could live on a tiny, remote island, at least for part of the year.

Finley called me Duchess, for reasons I had yet to decipher. To be fair, the nickname carried some validity. I was accustomed to luxury.

My condo back in Atlanta had been featured in magazines. Still, I didn't *need* all that to be happy. Days like today filled me with content. I was a citizen of the world. Though I had traveled widely, there were still places to go and people to see.

When my stomach began to growl, signaling the dinner hour, I toyed with the idea of staying in town to prove a point. I didn't have to rely on Finley's largesse. I was an independent woman.

On further reflection, I knew I'd be cutting off my nose to spite my face. There was no good reason not to go back. I anticipated the delivery of my new rental car. I needed my suitcases from the trunk of the old one. And I very much *wanted* to spend the evening with Finley.

Chapter 9

I ate shepherd's pie alone.

Finley's note on the kitchen table was short and direct: *The food is hot. I've gone to get your car and your things. Be back soon.*

Tamping down my disappointment, I served myself a generous helping of the casserole, poured a glass of milk, and sat down to my supper. The meal was astonishingly good. Except for my seafood meal last night, I'd not been overly impressed with Scottish cuisine up until now. Finley's housekeeper, though, was a culinary queen. The chunks of chicken were moist and savory. The broccoli and carrots and potatoes were neither crisp nor soggy. Even better, Finley's unseen employee had managed the perfect ratio of vegetables to meat. And the crust…oh, the crust! Golden brown. Flaky. My stomach did a high five. I'd have to walk a few extra miles this week to offset the rich, calorie-laden treat.

By seven, I had finished my meal and tidied the kitchen. Still no sign of Finley nor Cinnamon. Clearly, the man didn't trust me around his dog.

At seven thirty, I began to juggle anger and worry.

At seven forty-five, the back door opened along with a flurry of wind-driven leaves and a galloping spaniel. "You're back," I said. *Wow.* My conversational expertise had dried up entirely. I wasn't immune to the spark of sexual interest between Finley and me, but it was pretty clear that neither of us was interested in pursuing the attraction.

My host shrugged out of a light jacket and tossed keys on the kitchen table. "These are your new ones. I parked the car right outside. Pretty much like the one you had before, except this one is black."

My first rental had been a dull beige, so that wasn't altogether a bad trade. "How did you get out there?" He surely hadn't walked.

"Hamish gave me a lift. He owed me one for dragging his sorry hide home to his wife one night in June when he closed down the bars. He had just been told the little woman was expecting, and the news made him a wee bit agitated."

I grinned, imagining the enormous Hamish quaking at the thought of a tiny baby. "Please thank him when you see him again."

Finley nodded. He must have been starving, because he rummaged in the fridge for the shepherd's pie and held it up like a prize. "I've been looking forward to this all day."

"Would you like me to heat it for you while you wash up?"

"I know how to use a microwave, Duchess. But thanks."

Again, that sharp edge telling me not to overstep unseen boundaries. His sarcasm lit the fuse of my temper. "Is it me in particular you dislike? Or simply having your routine disturbed?"

If I thought plain speaking was going to rattle him, I was way off course.

At first, he said nothing. He simply busied himself heating a plate of food, gathering cutlery and a napkin, and popping open a beer. When he had his meal prepared to his satisfaction, he sat down and stared at me. "Stay or go. Don't hover."

I wanted badly to walk out of the room and leave him to his lonely meal. The only thing stopping me was a contrary inclination to do the exact opposite of what he wanted. Plus, I was curious, damn it.

Pulling out a chair with exaggerated care, I sat down and watched him eat. He attacked his food with single-minded relish. Did he only get home-cooked meals once a week when the housekeeper came?

The thought of Finley eating peanut butter sandwiches on cold, wintry evenings made me sad, which was ludicrous. Not every single man was helpless. Most of them enjoyed their lifestyles, despite the lack of services a wife might provide.

Though I loved to cook, I vowed then and there not to let myself be swayed by sympathy for a very happy bachelor. Finley Craig didn't need apple pies from me, nor warm cinnamon rolls on a chilly Highland morning.

As I watched him eat, I held my tongue, expecting him at any moment to answer my question. Either he had forgotten what I said or he didn't intend to respond, so I tried again. "Have I done something to offend you?" I asked. "You seem to be a reluctant Samaritan at best. Tell me. I really want to know. Is it my imagination, or do I annoy you in some way?"

With a sigh, he finished his last bite, wiped his mouth, and drained his beer. Twisting the brown glass bottle between long masculine fingers, he studied me. "Aye. You do. It's not your fault. I've not had a good experience with women like you."

"Women like me?" I frowned.

He clarified. "Blond. Gorgeous. Loaded."

In another circumstance, part of that description might have been complimentary. The grimace on his face took away any pleasure in the first two adjectives. My stomach churned. I'd never been dismissed quite so succinctly. "I see."

"I doubt ye do, lass. It's my problem. Not yours."

I shoved back from the table and stood up, righting my chair as it wobbled wildly. "Thank you for retrieving my rental car. Good night, Mr. Craig." My throat was tight and my eyes burned. I'd often been judged and found lacking by people in my life, but Finley's derision stung badly.

Before I could storm out of the room, he grabbed my wrist. "Don't run, lassie. I'll behave."

"Why should I stay where I'm not wanted?"

Our eyes met, his bright blue gaze locking with my brown, wary one. Absently, he rubbed the back of my wrist with his thumb, as if he'd forgotten he was holding me. "Don't be coy, McKenzie. You're a sophisticated woman. You know when a man wants you."

Oh, lordy. My throat closed up and my thighs clenched. Arousal, hot and sweet, flooded my abdomen. "Is that what this is?" I challenged him, wanting the truth. Needing confirmation.

"It is, and it's not. I'm far past the age where I act on every hormonal reaction to a woman's smile."

"How reassuring." Confusion and hurt made me snappy.

"Sit down, McKenzie. I'll tell you my sad tale, and maybe it will keep both of us from doing something stupid."

I let myself be persuaded...mostly because he was spot on about wanting to do something stupid. For a dollar, I'd consign old Cedric's house to the garbage collectors, and I'd hole up here in Portree with the fascinating but apparently unavailable Finley.

He released my wrist. I subsided into my chair and wrapped my arms around my waist. My chest still hurt the same way it used to when my father criticized my report cards or my friends.

"I'm listening." I wasn't prepared to cut him any slack. The man was a beast. A gorgeous, sexy, almost-but-not-quite adorable beast. He had bruised my feelings.

I sensed that he already regretted what he had said. The hour was late, the kitchen shadowy. Neither of us moved to turn on the lights.

Cinnamon snoozed in the corner, apparently unconcerned that her master was a horse's ass.

To keep from staring at my companion, I let my gaze drift around the old-fashioned kitchen. A small photograph on the wall caught my eye. In it, a teenage boy had his arm around a much younger girl. There was a strong family resemblance between the two. What I zeroed in on was something very familiar about the picture. Behind the two teenagers was a neon marquee recognizable to everyone in the developed world. The photo had been taken in Times Square. Although the Craigs might have done some traveling overseas, I didn't think that was the case in this instance.

Finally, the thing that had niggled at my subconscious for a full day now made sense. Finley's accent was a little different than most of the people I had met. A certain way of phrasing things. "You're not Scottish at all, are you?"

I felt betrayed and embarrassed for reasons Finley had no hint about. How could he know I was in search of my own Jamie Fraser?

He leaned back in his chair and rubbed his chin. "No. I'm not. Is that a problem?"

"Of course not," I lied. "I'm merely surprised. You don't sound American, not exactly. Then again, you don't talk like your neighbors either."

"I've lived here a decade. 'Tis not surprising that I've picked up some of the lingo."

Ah, life wasn't fair. Hadn't I learned that lesson a hundred different ways? I'd come to Scotland for a great adventure and in search of a man who was romantic and dashing and *different.* Instead, Finley was just another American. Expatriate or no, he wasn't my hero.

"I should go," I said. "And leave you in peace." Oddly, I didn't move.

Finley's intense gaze seemed to settle on the rise and fall of my breasts as I breathed deeply. "A man doesn't like admitting his mistakes."

"Then don't," I said sharply. "I'm not trying to drag secrets out of you. Believe me. I have my own problems. Feel free to keep your twisted past private."

He laughed out loud. And oh, the transformation. Grumpy Finley was a gorgeous hunk of man. Smiling Finley was *lethal.* I actually caught my breath. If a woman could spend the next fifty years making the man light up like that, she'd be darned lucky. It was hard work, but the results were magical.

Leaning his chair back on two legs, Finley laced his hands over his flat belly. "What problems could you possibly have, Duchess? Other than a rat-hole of a house and a wrecked car…both of which are temporary."

"Money doesn't buy happiness," I pointed out primly.

"But it's way ahead of what's in second place," Finley said. My host shook his head. "Are you telling me you aren't happy?"

I'd never really thought about it in those terms. "Of course I'm happy. Why wouldn't I be?"

He held up his hands. "Fine. You're happy. I get it. Let's back up. Tell me why you came to Scotland."

"You have to promise not to laugh."

"Scout's honor."

Now, *that* sounded American. "Have you heard of a television show called *Outlander*? Or even the books?"

Finley winced. "Lord, yes."

"What does that mean?"

He pointed to the photograph I'd been studying earlier. "My baby sister, Bella, is a full-fledged *Outlander* fanatic. She's five years younger than I am and a voracious reader. She knows the books inside and out and has seen every episode of the show half a dozen times. Her dearest wish is to move to Scotland and live with me."

"So why doesn't she?"

"Bella is a brainiac. She's has two Master's degrees in English Literature and Medieval Studies and is working on a PhD in European History."

"So she can move here with you…"

"That's the plan." He shrugged. "We're close now, but as a big brother I let her down a dozen ways growing up. She excelled, and I was the screw-up."

"You don't strike me as a miserable failure." That was the closest he was going to get to a compliment from me tonight. He was the kind of man who drove women to make fools of themselves. Handsome and charming and bad to the bone. I knew instinctively to be on my guard around him, in the same way I knew that the German Shepherd down the block from my condo in Atlanta was to be given a wide berth.

Finley, oblivious to my soul searching, shook his head. "I was kicked out of a dozen prep schools in the northeast before Bella was eight years old. My father took a belt to me on a regular basis, but somehow, it never helped. When Bella was old enough, she would sneak into my bedroom at night and try to convince me to study. I was a lost cause. My counselor said my IQ was too high, and I wasn't being challenged in school." His laugh held little humor. "The truth is, I was a punk-ass adolescent who needed to be taken down several notches."

"Did that happen eventually?"

"Not really. It finally occurred to me that if I didn't get into a good school and make something of myself, I'd be living under my father's roof forever. That was too dismal a prospect to endure. I eventually graduated from the last of the prep academies, got accepted at the university of my choice, and spent the next six years turning my life around. I finished with an engineering degree and an MBA. Bella cried her eyes out when I was done."

"She sounds like a very special person."

"Aye, she is. Enough about Bella. Why the Outlander question?"

It was my turn to wince. "My two best friends and I are much like your sister in our Outlander obsession. We came to the Highlands together for a month, but split up so we could have our own adventures."

"That seems odd...doesn't it?"

"Not at all. We're each staying at various places in the area. We'll meet up again before going home. In the meantime, we wanted to immerse ourselves in Scotland...to become locals, if you will."

"I see. And what does this grand scheme have to do with Outlander? Other than location."

For half a second I searched for a believable lie. This man already held a poor opinion of me. No doubt, the idea of searching for true love would reinforce his notion that I was a lightweight. What the hell; I wasn't going to apologize for who I was. I'd spent a lot of time with my shrink learning to step out of my parents' shadows and expectations.

So I told him the truth.

Chapter 10

With every bit of storytelling wizardry I could muster, I gave Finley a synopsis of the first Outlander book. “So you see,” I said, “my friends and I are here to walk in the steps of Claire Randall.”

“A fictional character…” He seemed dubious.

“Fictional, yes. Yet real in that she embodies emotions and experiences that are universal for women. We can’t go back in time, of course, but we set some parameters for our adventure.”

“I’m almost afraid to ask.” He was definitely interested. I could see it in those brilliant blue eyes.

“For the next month, we’re going tech-free. Except in dire emergencies, no cell phones, no Internet, no Facebook. You get the drift.”

“And if you need to contact your friends?”

“Every night at nine o’clock we turn on our phones and check for messages. If any of us has a problem, we text 9-1-1.” I didn’t mention the fact that I’d be using my computer and my photo editing software to work on my photography. I wouldn’t be online, so that activity met the letter of the law.

“How does the Jamie Fraser fellow fit into all this?”

Damn. The man *had* been paying attention. “Well, um…”

Finley rolled his eyes. “You want to fall in love with a Scotsman—right?”

I stared at him and lifted my chin. “I’m open to the idea. So, yes. Searching for romance and Mr. Right wasn’t a crime the last time I checked.”

“Not at all.”

His expression was grave. I had a hunch he was laughing at me on the inside.

"Go ahead," I said glumly. "Make fun of me. I can take it."

"Not at all. In fact, I think I can help."

* * * * * * * **

Half an hour later, I found myself taking a brisk walk with my host and a very well-behaved Cinnamon. After Finley dropped his conversational bomb at the kitchen table, it became clear that the puppy was ready to be taken out. At my request, Finley had waited for me to run upstairs and change clothes. He'd already carried my suitcases to my room. It took a matter of moments to grab a pair of jeans, top them with a mauve linen tunic and gold chain, and slide my feet into espadrilles. I was so sick of wearing that white pantsuit I'd probably shove it in a closet for the duration of the trip.

Finley didn't appear to pay much attention to clothes…but then again, he didn't have to. Whatever he wore, whether black leather or gray wool or a simple navy T-shirt, suited him. This evening it was old denims and a button up shirt in cream with a tiny black check.

Now that I was no longer wearing heels, the difference in our heights was magnified. He was a tall man and had a long stride. With Cinnamon straining at the leash, I had to walk quickly to keep up. Unlike last night, I was full of energy. I loved the Scottish summer of a warm day followed by a cool night. The climate was invigorating.

Or maybe it was the company.

As we rounded the first bend in the road, we halted where Cinnamon and I had stopped the night before to look at the view. "Have you always lived in your current house?" I asked. I had questions aplenty, but also doubts about how forthcoming Finley might be. He seemed in a mellow mood at the moment, so I decided to satisfy my curiosity.

He squatted to praise Cinnamon for not chasing after a rabbit. "Good girl." Glancing up at me, he nodded. "Pretty much. When I first came out here from the States, I had been camping out in the used car I bought in Edinburgh. I had a nest egg to start my business. Didn't want to blow it on lodging. When I made it as far as Portree, something about the place caught my imagination."

"So you bought a house?"

"Who's telling this story? You or me?"

"Sorry." I kicked at a stick and put my hands in my pockets.

"I saw an ad in the window of one of the pubs in town. It was from an old guy who needed help in exchange for room and board."

"And you accepted."

"Aye, I did. The arrangement suited us both. I was young and strong and didn't mind fixing broken furniture and appliances, doing outside chores, cutting back trees…anything like that."

"Where is he now?"

I saw his shoulders tense the slightest bit. I only noticed because I was above him.

"He died. Four years ago. Left his crazy old house to me. I couldn't accept, of course. The authorities found a daughter down in England. She hadn't seen the old man in a decade. Didn't even make it north for the funeral. The solicitors contacted her and explained the situation. She sent a letter abandoning all claim to the estate."

"Why?"

"I suppose she had a falling out with her father. And she probably knew there were debts."

"So that's how you became a Scottish landowner."

"In a nutshell, yes."

I sensed there was more he wasn't saying, but I let the subject drop in favor of a more pressing one. "You mentioned something about helping me meet Scottish men?"

Finley groaned. "I'm starting to regret it now."

"No take-backs," I teased. "I'm going to be living in a remote house all alone, so my social life will need all the help it can get."

"Fine. I know several single blokes who would be more than happy to meet you. I'll throw together something for tomorrow night. Hamish has a big room he rents out upstairs over the restaurant. He'll give it to me for no charge since it's a weeknight. Some drinks, a wee bit of food and music, and we'll be good to go."

"Wait a minute," I said, incredulous. "Are you actually going to organize an entire event for me?"

"Not really organized." Finley's lazy smile was at my expense, no doubt. "More of an impromptu ceilidh. Around here we love our parties. And while we're on the subject, I need to know your parameters."

"Parameters?" I parroted the word.

"You know. Age. Height. Weight. I already know he has to be a Scotsman. You made that abundantly clear."

I narrowed my eyes at him, but Finley didn't back down. Had I insulted my host by taking him out of the running? Was he actually going through with this idea? Or was it all an elaborate scheme to pull my leg? "I don't have parameters," I insisted. "Well, maybe age. I'm thirty-two, so anything from thirty to forty-five would be acceptable."

"Duly noted. What about red hair? Your Jamie Fraser crush has red hair, doesn't he?"

"I'm not looking to meet a Jamie Fraser clone," I insisted. "All I'm interested in is finding someone who is Scottish, a gentleman, and fun to be with. Not that I'm expect him to entertain me 24/7. I'm here in the Highlands to expand my horizons. A bit of romance on the side is merely the icing on the cake."

This was an odd game of chicken we were playing. Finley pretending to pimp me out to his friends at a party, and me giving every appearance of agreeing. One of us had to back down. Unluckily for Finley, I was as stubborn as they came. If he was going to perpetuate this ludicrous idea, then I sure as heck would let it ride.

I couldn't wait to see the look on his face when he admitted he'd only been yanking my chain. That would be priceless.

We turned for the stroll back up the hill. Though we hadn't gone far, the air held a noticeable chill now. I wrapped my arms around myself and shivered. The prospect of staying in Cedric's damp, cold house was not appealing at all, especially now that I had made myself at home with Finley and Cinnamon.

Nevertheless, I'd be moving out very soon. Maybe even tomorrow evening if Mrs. Clark and her daughter were miracle workers.

In Finley's kitchen once again, I felt a sudden awkwardness. He'd never mentioned the blond and gorgeous comment again. Now I had waited too long to push for an answer. I was very conscious of infringing upon his time and his good nature. Plus, I didn't want to be teased anymore about the party full of eligible men. "I think I'll head upstairs," I said.

"So soon?"

We both glanced at the clock. It wasn't even nine. "I'm sure you have things to do," I said, the words stilted. "And I want to write a few postcards I picked up today."

I was not imagining the level of sexual tension in the room. It was as if our bodies were carrying out a seductive conversation that had nothing to do with politeness or social propriety.

Finley was right. I *did* know when a man wanted me. And there he stood, only an arm's length away.

Poor Cinnamon had been consigned to the study again. Without the dog to run interference, now it was just Finley and me. I found myself getting all hot and bothered. My pulse rate accelerated. My breathing fractured. My hands were cold as ice. "Goodnight," I muttered, as for the second time I prepared to leave.

"Don't go."

The words were hoarse. I was almost certain Finley hadn't meant to say them. They were sincere. Not teasing. Not condescending.

I took my time answering. Because it was important I get this right. "Why would I stay?"

The table was between us. Nice and strong for whatever antics humans might think up to do. Finley lifted one shoulder in a graceful, masculine shrug. "We'll drink together. Up on the roof. How does that sound? You're all about fitting in and learning the local culture. You need to know and love whiskey."

A smile tugged at my lips. "That's all it takes to be a Scot?"

"It's a start."

I didn't know what we were doing. Well, I *did* know we were flirting, but I didn't know why. Finley had some sort of chip on his shoulder about me. I, on the other hand, knew that this dark angel, this leather-clad bad boy had the power to derail my trip to Scotland.

Still, it was only a drink between acquaintances. No harm in that. "Okay," I said. "A drink sounds nice."

Finley grabbed a bottle of amber liquid and a couple of glasses. Then he led me on an excursion up through the various levels of his whimsical house. When we reached the attic, he lowered a set of stairs. "Up you go."

It was uncomfortable shimmying up the ladder and knowing his eyes were on a level with my butt. He was carrying stuff, so maybe he was too preoccupied to notice. In the attic, the air was noticeably cooler. There wasn't much insulation and vents on either end let in the night air.

"One more climb," Finley said.

This time he went first. The ladder was straight up, not on a slant. At the top, Finley reached up and pushed at a storm-cellar type of door. It creaked and groaned but finally flopped to one side. Now I could see stars.

"Doesn't it leak in the rain?" I asked as I looked up from below.

"Sometimes. Hold on." Finley disappeared only to return a few seconds later without the whiskey and glasses. He extended his arm in my direction. "Come on up, Duchess."

Chapter 11

Finley's rooftop was no fancy penthouse garden on the Upper East Side. It did have two ancient lawn chairs and a rickety quasi-table. He escorted me to my seat and joined me opposite the small wooden bench, then poured us each a glass of whiskey.

When he passed me my drink, our fingers touched. It seemed as if sparks flickered from the simple contact. This was all wrong. I was supposed to be pursuing my photography and learning things about Scotland, not having rooftop trysts with the kind of man who broke hearts as a sport.

Well, that wasn't fair. If there were hearts being broken, the women were partly to blame. They should have known better. Not even the most naïve female on the planet could convince herself that Finley Craig was boyfriend or husband material.

The whiskey, though I sipped it slowly, burned in the pit of my stomach. Gradually, the warmth spread outward to my limbs. I rested my head on the back of the chair and looked at the sky. So many stars. I never saw the sky like this in Atlanta...or even New York for that matter.

Far below me, the town slept. Portree was a gem of a place. I loved it already. "What does the name mean?" I asked.

"It's pronounced *Port Righ,* which translates as king's port, but in older documents, it's Port *Ruighe,* or sloped harbor, so take your pick."

"I like the second one," I said. "Do you speak any Gaelic?"

"Only the occasional word or phrase. It's a wee bit difficult to learn."

"I'm sure it must be." The signs I'd seen on my way to the island were written in both English and Gaelic. As far as I could tell, there was little point in common between the two.

After half an hour or so, Finley refilled his glass. I still nursed my drink. I didn't like feeling out of control. Between Finley and the alcohol and the beautiful night, I was in danger of floating off into space.

"Are you asleep over there?" he asked with a smile in his voice.

"Almost." Might as well be honest.

"We've talked way too much about me. Tell me what a Duchess does when she's back home in her native land."

I took another sip of whiskey. "I have a degree in interior design." I said it bluntly, waiting for him to criticize.

"Why did you choose that?"

"Well, I suppose it's because I respect beauty in all its forms. Beauty adds meaning to life. It can also make life bearable."

"So you help wealthy Georgia debutantes decorate their mansions?"

The over-the-top stereotype made me smile. I wasn't ashamed of my debutante days. "That's part of it." I didn't tell him more for fear he would think I was bragging.

"Scotland is beautiful. Is that why you came?"

Again, I equivocated. "One reason, yes. Though beyond the beauty, there's magic, I think. History, tragic and triumphant. A land torn by war and built on the blood of its people. Hayley and Willow and I wanted to experience that for ourselves. As an outsider, you probably understand."

"Aye. The hills here are old and wise. Progress is slow and measured. The natural world is a resource to be cossetted and not crushed."

"Will you ever move back?"

"I doubt it. At least not until my father is gone."

"I don't understand."

He leaned forward, elbows on his knees, and bowed his head. "I don't expect you to. It's a long, ugly story, and it's late. You need to go back inside and go to bed."

"What about you?"

He turned to face me, though I couldn't read his expression in the dark. "Is that an invitation, lass?"

The unaccustomed alcohol had lowered my inhibitions. Finley was a rare, fascinating creature. I wanted to wallow in him. At the last second, I found my good sense. "Not at all. Just a question."

"You go first. I'll be down in a bit."

"Suddenly you're trying to get rid of me."

He cursed, the words a combination of Gaelic and English. "I have a hard-on, ye daft lass. If I go downstairs with you, we'll end up in your bed or mine. Is that what you want?"

His blunt speaking flooded my face with heat. "Of course not," I muttered. "I barely know you." I fled with the sound of his mocking laughter ringing in my ears.

* * * *

The following morning, I awoke to another note on the kitchen table:

Don't try to move to Cedric's house today. Even if the ladies finish cleaning, it will be late. We have the party tonight. Tomorrow morning you can shop for provisions and get settled in at your new place.

Rain is on the way, so you should get in some sightseeing today. I'll be working, but be ready to leave the house at seven. Wear something that shows a bit of skin. The lads will like that.

I read the words three times before crumpling the paper in my hand. My host was high-handed, bossy, and way too inclined to have his own way. The infuriating thing was he was right. About all of it. So to fly in the face of his orders—thinly veiled as advice—would serve no purpose at all.

Mumbling to myself, I gobbled down a light breakfast and hurried back upstairs to finish getting ready. If the weather was about to turn ugly, I should get out and about with my camera.

It felt good to have transportation again. And luggage. And all my things. I'd be driving only in the daylight, so there should be nothing to worry about. I packed a tote with water and snacks and a guidebook, and set out. I had a couple of options. Since I was going to be on Skye for an entire month, I could use today to get my bearings with one big, long looping drive around the island. Without stops.

On the other hand, I could begin closer to home. According to my book, there was a famous waterfall not far from town, fifteen miles maybe. Mealt Falls at Kilt Rock sounded like an auspicious place to start my month of Scottish photography.

The day was picture perfect. Blue skies, abundant sunshine. It was hard to believe more rain was on the way, but I knew that blustery weather was the norm here. Fortunately, I had no problems navigating the winding road. Now I could see everything I had missed the day I arrived.

Though I hoped it wouldn't be a faux pas, I stopped by my rental house to meet Mrs. Clark and her crew. Already they had made a dent in the considerable job. I thanked them profusely and made arrangements to pay when they were done. With the sun on my face and Cedric's house beginning to look a bit more palatable, my spirits lifted.

My month in Scotland had gotten off to a rocky start, but I would soon be back on track.

Though I kept stopping for photographs, I eventually arrived at my destination. It was late in the season. Even so, a handful of tourists milled about in the small car park. I grabbed up my camera case and locked the vehicle. I planned on being extra cautious today. I didn't want to create any situation from which I might have to be rescued.

The waterfall over the Kilt Rock formation was breathtaking. It plunged at least fifty feet into the ocean below. Beyond the falls, dramatic headlands carved by centuries of wind and water jutted against the sky.

I was in heaven.

Quickly deciding what lens to use, I changed it out and readied my camera. An iron railing set back from the edge a few feet was a clear attempt to keep foolish tourists from accidentally falling. It was the same the world over, but I hoped the safety feature wasn't going to interfere with my shots.

I realized right away that the polite thing to do was wait my turn. There was one spot where the falls could be framed to best advantage, but everyone had the same idea.

My patience paid off in the end. One group at a time piled into cars, and soon, I was all alone. I knew it wouldn't last. This was a very popular place. In the meantime, I was going to take advantage of my good luck.

Back in Atlanta, I'd practiced changing out various lenses and filters. I was now able to move from one to the other rapidly. I wondered if it were possible to take a bad picture under such circumstances. Here I was, standing at an overlook of one of the most impressive waterfalls I had even seen, and there was nothing to mar my enjoyment or my view.

I was almost finished shooting when I noticed a single yellow wildflower clinging to the grass at the edge of the cliff just beyond the guardrail. There was actually enough room for an adult to crouch on the grass there, but to do so would be suicidal. Even the thought of it made my stomach curl.

Debating my options, I set about to capture the shot without plunging to my death. I could see the headlines now: *Foolish American tourist dies in search of a flower.*

What I wanted was a shot with the flower in the foreground and the magnificent waterfall softly blurred in the background. Framed with the ocean and the sky, the green cliffs would be even more powerful and impressive.

The problem was vantage point. Both the waterfall and the flower were on the same plane. I studied the situation, trying to call up my faint memories of geometry. At last I decided it might work.

Unfortunately, the ground was still muddy from early days of rain. I was going to get very dirty, but I was determined not to leave without this one picture.

I walked to the far end of the viewing area, away from the waterfall. Then I gradually returned, keeping my eye on the brave yellow flower and the water in the distance. When I determined that the moment was right, I sat down in the goopy grass and eased one arm and shoulder past the guardrail. I still had three fourths of my body on terra firma. I looped one leg around a post as insurance.

Anyone could drive up at any moment and ruin my effort. I was trying to hurry without being careless. After pausing to make sure the camera strap was securely around my neck, I leaned out as far as I could and craned to get the shot. The camera was heavy. I needed to support the camera with both hands, but I couldn't do that and hold onto the post at the same time.

Carefully, I let go and balanced the camera until I had a comfortable grip. I was in no danger of falling, as my leg was wrapped around the post. My right elbow was propped on the grass just past the guardrail. Really, it wasn't risky at all.

Peering through the lens, I felt excitement flood my stomach. This was a shot in a million. One tiny brave flower clinging to life with the powerful waterfall in the background. The sun beamed down on me, making me sweat. I was determined to take advantage of an opportunity that might never again be this perfect during the month I was here.

Vertical. Horizontal. Haze filter. Polarizer. I must have taken a hundred shots. Maybe more. Unfortunately, my body was beginning to protest the awkward position. Even my yoga training couldn't help the fact that my right arm was tingling.

I hadn't really thought about the ramifications of getting up. As I was pondering how to keep my camera safe while backing away from a sheer cliff and a deadly drop-off, I registered the sound of a car door and footsteps drawing nearer. Drat. My solitude was over. At least I had accomplished my goal.

As I was easing back from the edge, a male voice intruded on my artistic introspection.

"What in the hell are you doing?"

Chapter 12

Finley. Of course. Why did he always have to catch me in compromising positions? I scooted my butt backward, wincing when pieces of gravel bit into my hip. "Take this," I said, holding up the camera. "Be careful with it."

Without the heavy piece of equipment, it was a lot easier to grab the guardrail and lever myself to a standing position. I brushed off my pants and wiped my hands on my shirttail. "Thanks," I said.

When I looked up, his expression was thunderous. "Do you have a death wish?" he demanded. "Are you that reckless with your life?"

"Oh, pooh," I said. "I was perfectly safe. Don't be such an alarmist."

He pointed to the red-and-white sign with the stick figure of a person tumbling off the cliff. "They put these warnings here for a reason."

"I wasn't standing. I was sitting. And I was hanging on tightly. I got the most amazing pictures." I wanted to dance around in celebration, but Finley didn't share my enthusiasm.

"Most tourists use an iPhone," he pointed out, sounding grumpy. Was he pale beneath his tan? It was hard to tell.

"What are you doing here?" I asked. "Aren't you supposed to be in your workshop playing with exhaust pipes and handlebars?"

"It occurred to me I didn't have much in the way of food in the house when you left. I stopped to pick up some meat pies and blueberry scones. I thought we might have a picnic."

I stared at him. "Why are you being nice?"

A smile tugged at his lips. "Am I? Being nice, that is?"

Nodding, I grimaced at the state of my clothes. "You are. Suspiciously so. My mother taught me to beware Greeks bearing gifts."

He saluted. "American, remember? Don't be so paranoid. Maybe I wanted to take advantage of this beautiful day."

When a man offers a woman a picnic, he generally has one thing on his mind. Since I was starving, I decided to ignore the subtext and satisfy my hunger. At least the hunger that could be appeased with savory food and yummy dessert.

I had yet to see a picnic table. Did they even have them in Scotland? "Where are we going to sit?"

"How about the hood of your car?"

It was a good choice given the state of the ground. I was already dirty though, so it wouldn't have mattered. Still, the hood was warm from the sun and we had room to spread out the food between us. Finley had included a couple of apples as well. He pulled out a pocketknife and offered me one piece at a time as he cut them.

"Good apple," I mumbled. Something about having a man feed me fruit was almost as intimate as kissing. His hand to my lips...that kind of thing.

Finley finished off the last slice and put the core back in the paper sack. "So what's this obsession with thrill-seeking photography?" he asked.

"You build motorcycles. I take pictures. I'd like to be good enough to have an exhibition of my work. It excites me. I thought about getting an MFA, but I like the challenge of figuring out things on my own."

"Are you any good?"

Even with his sunglasses on, I could tell he was teasing. "I'm no Ansel Adams, but I'm getting there."

With my belly full and my artistic drive appeased for the moment, I leaned back on my elbows and closed my eyes. I'd covered my exposed skin with sunscreen earlier, so I let the hot rays soak into my face without guilt. Nothing felt as good as basking in the sun with the breeze lifting my hair and the sound of the ocean far in the distance.

When I sneaked a peek beneath my lashes, I saw that Finley, too, was sun-worshipping. Except that he had reclined against the windshield and laced his hands over his flat abdomen. I studied him surreptitiously. His profile was classic; only a small silver scar on the bottom of his chin marred perfection.

His hair was a deep, glossy black that shone in the sun. It was his lips that intrigued me the most. Full and sensual, they belonged to a man who lived life fully, in all its wonderful, messy extravagant emotional chaos.

If I could have reached my camera, I would have photographed him exactly like this. I didn't know what to make of Finley. He seemed full of secrets and contradictions.

I wasn't averse to the idea of a vacation romance. I'd wanted to meet my version of Jamie Fraser. Finley wasn't it. Even so, it would be fun to have a companion occasionally as I explored the island.

He slept now, deeply, peacefully. I wanted to reach over and unbutton his shirt…to feel his smooth belly and trace the ribs beneath his golden skin.

My pulse raced. I'd rarely felt such an immediate physical attraction. In the beginning, when I assumed he was a Scotsman, there was some excuse for my fascination. But Finley was a plain old American. Not exotic at all. Should I let this zing between us run its course, or should I hold out for a real hero?

He stirred and looked at me, his eyelids heavy. "What are you thinking about, Duchess? Your face is all flushed."

I sat up and put my hands to my cheeks. "It's the sun," I said. "I'm so fair-skinned I turn pink in no time."

"Hmpf." He closed his eyes again.

My explanation was only half the truth. I couldn't exactly tell him I was fantasizing about undressing him. I reached for my water bottle and drained the last of it. "Shouldn't you get back to work?" I said.

This time he kept his eyes closed. "I never take a day off. This is nice. What's your hurry?"

"Well for one, I have to pee."

My honesty caught him off guard, and he burst out laughing. His humor at my expense made me cross. "It's not funny. You can go anywhere. Back home we have trees and bushes in the great outdoors. There's not much cover around here."

Finley sat up and wiped his eyes. "Ah, Duchess. You're an original. Why don't you hop back to Cedric's place and use the facilities?"

"I didn't think of that."

"You *are* paying for it."

"True." The longer he stayed, the more I was tempted to do something far more stupid than hanging near a precipitous ledge and taking a photograph.

"I'm going to leave now," I said politely. *If you'll get off the hood of my car.*

He didn't take the hint. "I'll watch for other cars," he said. There's no one for miles around. Feel free to take care of business."

"Oh, no," I said, shaking my head. "With my luck, a busload of tourists would pull up at exactly the wrong moment. I'll go back to Cedric's. I need you to move, please."

He slid off the car and stretched, extending his arms toward the sky. "You're such a spoilsport. I'll head back. Promise me one thing."

"What?"

"Try not to put yourself in other dangerous situations. We have rocks and cliffs and bogs. Stay out of trouble."

His condescending attitude was a bit much. "I wasn't in any trouble *this* time," I said. "But thanks for the warning."

The sarcastic tone was impossible to miss, even for a deluded male. His jaw jutted forward. "You seem to attract trouble, Duchess. How are your knees, by the way?"

Truthfully, they stung like the devil. I wasn't about to admit that to him. "No worries." I paused to remember my manners. "Thank you for feeding me. It wasn't necessary, but I appreciate it."

He grinned. "You don't like accepting help, do you?"

"I'm used to getting by on my own," I answered, avoiding a direct answer. It was true. I wasn't a Kardashian or anything, but around Atlanta, people knew who I was. A Southern heiress was so clichéd. Sometimes it felt as if I walked around with a dollar sign over my head. So maybe I overcompensated by making sure any success I had was my own.

Finally, Finley straddled his motorcycle and donned his helmet. "I'll see you back at the house," he said.

I nodded. "I'll be there."

As he drove away, I jumped in the car and followed, though I turned off at the drive up to the McCracken place. Mrs. Clark greeted me with a frown. Maybe she thought I was checking up on her. When I expressed a dire need for the restroom, her expression cleared.

The women had done an amazing job already. All the windows in the house were open to air things out, and the heat was running to take care of any lingering moisture. The beds had been stripped. The laundry, hanging on clotheslines, flapped in the breeze as it dried.

Soon, this little cottage would be all mine. For weeks I had looked forward to my solitary getaway. Nothing but time and space on my hands to think and to exercise and to read books. It had sounded like heaven. And it still did; only now I felt a twinge of regret at having to move out of Finley's house.

I was only beginning to know him. When I moved up here on the hillside, I wouldn't be able to use my cell phone per my agreement with Hayley and Willow, even if I could get a signal. Hopefully, Cedric had a landline that would be my connection to Finley and to Portree.

After thanking Mrs. Clark again for her willingness to tackle such a big job, I headed back down the rutted track to the main road. For the rest of the afternoon, I was going to drive without stopping.

I kept my promise to myself. Mostly. At times I simply *had* to pull off and take a picture through my open window. In some places the road skirted the edge of the island offering magnificent ocean views. Elsewhere, like the Quiraing, where a massive Jurassic landslip created strange and beautiful rock formations, the scenery was mountainous and impressive.

There would be plenty to keep me busy for the month, though I hadn't expected the island to be quite so devoid of people. If I were to keep my promise to my two friends and find an eligible Scotsman, it would have to happen in Portree, most likely. The other "towns" on Skye were little more than clusters of houses. Portree itself wasn't exactly a booming metropolis.

Even with an influx of visitors for the music festival, Skye was uncrowded and unspoiled. I loved it.

Around four thirty, I finished my long loop of the island and headed back to my starting point. Finley was nowhere to be seen when I arrived at his house. I slipped up to my room for a quick shower. After drying my hair, I sat in front of a small vanity and used a bit of mascara to give some definition to my pale lashes.

Deciding what to wear was surprisingly challenging. I'd brought plenty of clothes; that wasn't the problem. I'd never been to a small-town ceilidh, so I didn't know what to expect.

After trying on and discarding three outfits, I settled for a dress. It was deceptively simple. When I put it on, it skimmed my body, hiding the extra curvy bottom I could never seem to fine-tune and emphasizing my narrow waist. The bodice was a halter-top. It fastened at the back of my neck with a single rhinestone clasp.

Though my shoulders and much of my back were bare, my cleavage was respectably covered. The hemline hit right above my knees. I decided it was warm enough to go barelegged. I abandoned my favorite heels in favor of silver ballet flats that would be suitable for dancing. With a light, filmy shawl and a small clutch purse, I was ready.

Ridiculously nervous, I went down to the kitchen at a quarter 'til seven. There would be food at the party. A good thing, because my stomach was growling. The picnic with Finley was hours ago.

I heard a noise behind me and turned to find my host staring at me, apparently gobsmacked. "Holy hell," he said.

Chapter 13

Putting a hand to my throat, I grimaced. "You said to show some skin. Is this dress too much?"

He swallowed visibly. "Well, it depends."

"What do you mean by that?"

"For a casual summer ceilidh, it's perfect. If you're feeling shy tonight, though, I think you're in trouble. Every unattached Scotsman in a twenty-five-mile radius will be drawn to you like bees to honey. With that southern accent and magnolia complexion, not to mention a dress designed to give a man ideas, you're a walking, talking fantasy."

"I should go change." His assessment made me nervous. I hated being the center of attention.

"Don't you dare. You told me that you and Hayley and Willow came to the Highlands to meet your own versions of Jamie Fraser. Tonight, you'll have all the available guinea pigs gathered in one place. 'Twill be like shooting fish in a barrel."

I frowned, shifting from one foot to the other. The inside of my cheek was raw where I had bitten it. I was starting to sweat even though it was perfectly pleasant outside. "I think you're making fun of me."

He held up his hands. "I wouldn't. I couldn't. We're going to dance the night away, McKenzie. I want you to enjoy yourself. They're a welcoming group. You'll have a wonderful evening."

* * * *

Beside the entrance to Hamish's lovely seafood restaurant was a second door that opened to a narrow flight of stairs. The tight space smelled vaguely of onions and fish. Despite first impressions, when we made it to the second floor and into the room Finley had described, I was enchanted.

In every window on the street side, single candles flickered in tall glass hurricane lamps. The walls were plain white plaster, the floor polished hardwood. I was fairly certain the boards beneath my feet must be over a hundred years old. It was hard to fake that kind of patina and wood grain.

At the far end of the room, a small band tuned their instruments. I saw three fiddles, a set of bagpipes, a guitar, and a small harp. To one side, a queue had already formed at the cash bar. Though we had arrived a few minutes early, the large room was filling rapidly.

As it turned out, I was right. Finley *had* been pulling my leg. He'd made me believe he was going to throw a party just for me. This ceilidh was a regular event. It was also the perfect opportunity for him to introduce me to his friends.

On one side of the room an enterprising carpenter had installed open wooden cubbies, the kind we used in kindergarten back home. As I watched, the women tucked away wraps and purses. It must be a very trusting crowd. Some even ditched their shoes. I wasn't much of a dancer at all, much less barefoot, so I kept my flats right where they belonged.

Along the wall opposite the cubbies, tables were lined up end to end bearing finger foods. When my stomach growled loudly, Finley chuckled. "What if I go stand in line to grab us drinks and you fix yourself a plate?"

"Oh, no," I said. "Don't leave me." The roomful of strangers was intimidating despite my fairly extensive social life back in the States. I knew the rules on Park Avenue, New York, and in Buckhead, Atlanta. The Isle of Skye was something else again.

"Then what first? Food or drink?"

"Food please," I said meekly.

Fortunately for my blood sugar, we managed to gobble down fish and chips and shortbread cookies before we were interrupted.

Finley looked up as a rotund man in his early thirties approached us with all the linear precision of a torpedo. "Here's number one," Finley whispered.

For a moment I didn't understand. And then it became clear. Now was the part of the evening where Finley trotted out a series of eligible Scotsmen. I smiled pleasantly as the stranger joined us.

I could swear Finley's eyes danced with laughter as he made the introductions. "McKenzie, I'd like you to meet my friend Tom Nickelson. Tom is a leading authority on genealogy. His specialty is the family histories of the Highlands."

"How interesting," I said politely. Tom was at least half a foot shorter than I was, even with me wearing flats. His broad face was shiny with perspiration, and he smelled like the stairwell.

Finley continued the formalities. "Tom, old buddy, this vision is McKenzie Taylor. She's here in the Highlands for a month vacationing. We haven't managed to make it to the bar yet. I'm sure she'd appreciate it if you would accompany her."

"Well, of course I will," Tom said, seemingly unfazed by the fact that I looked like his older, taller sister. "Come along now."

I shot Finley a murderous glance over my shoulder, but the expression on his face was bland innocence. After that, I lost sight of the only person in the room familiar to me.

Tom dragged me in his wake, making the crowd part from the sheer force of his determination. We must have looked like a tugboat pulling the Titanic. When we finally reached the bar, I was out of breath. Somehow, Tom finessed us to the front of the line.

I glanced apologetically at the men and women behind us. They rolled their eyes, clearly used to Tom's antics.

"What's your pleasure, Ms. Taylor?" Tom asked.

"Call me McKenzie, please. A rum and Coke would be nice."

He shook his head. "That's no good." He turned to the bartender. "We'll have two Glenfinnans. Neat."

The little twerp. His self-important assurance that he could override my choice was irritating. I swallowed my pique. I might as well get this over with. When we had our drinks, I allowed him to steer me once again, this time toward a corner of the room where the air was marginally cooler. Clearly, this entertainment space was not outfitted with air conditioning. Someone had started opening the large windows and letting in the late evening breeze. Even so, the press of bodies kept the temperature warm.

"So are you a native of Skye, Tom?"

"Born and raised here," he said proudly. "My lineage goes all the way back to before Culloden and the uprising. We're a mix of McDonalds and another clan that died out. I've had several papers published on the subject. I'm sure you would find them edifying. I'll make you copies and bring them to you. Where did you say you were staying?"

My spine tingled as my sleazeball-o-meter went off. "I didn't say," I muttered. "If you'll excuse me, I need to find the ladies room."

I abandoned the miniature Scotsman so fast, he never knew what happened. Standing on my tiptoes, I was able to spot Finley, only because he was head and shoulders over most of the partygoers. The music had started in earnest. The dance floor was getting crowded.

In a snit, I walked up to my American host and poked him in the chest with a finger. "You did that on purpose."

He lifted an eyebrow. "You said you wanted to meet interesting natives."

"Not funny, Mr. Craig. Not at all."

Before I could finish my tirade, another of Finley's friends stopped by, clearly angling for an introduction. This one was taller than me, but he was on the far end of the age range.

Finley shook hands with the man. "McKenzie, meet Jordan Darvon. Jordan, this is McKenzie Taylor from the States."

Jordan pumped my hand. He had the grip of a dead codfish. And Finley, darn him, had already disappeared, leaving me to my fate.

My new admirer gazed at me with soulful eyes. "I'm delighted to meet ye, young lady. My wife died of the cancer two years ago, and this is the first time I've been out to dance. I don't suppose you'd like to take a turn on the floor? You remind me a little bit of her, though she was smaller and had blue eyes, not brown. How long do you think a man should be on his own before he thinks of marrying again?"

I didn't even try to interrupt the monologue. When I found Finley this time, I was going to kill him. So help me God.

Jordan managed to talk nonstop about his dead wife for a solid half hour. I was a compassionate person. I even admired a man who still loved his wife so much. Still, listening to a stranger hit on me out of sheer loneliness was where I drew the line.

At long last, I managed to extricate myself from the forlorn widower. Unfortunately, Finley had shown the good sense to hide where I couldn't find him. I sat in a folding chair near the window and tapped my toe to the music. Most of the numbers were fast. I recognized the occasional upbeat American pop tune. For the most part, the band played traditional pieces. It wasn't a bad way to spend an evening.

I watched the crowd interact and had to smile. There seemed to be no age limit to "cutting a rug" at a ceilidh. I saw a couple who had to be in their eighties kicking up their heels in a dizzying reel. Then of course, there were all the adolescents mingling awkwardly and casting longing glances at the objects of their affections.

It was fun. I might have had more fun were Hayley and Willow with me, but maybe not. We probably would have chosen to take a walk in the dark instead of inserting ourselves in something that was so uniquely local and authentic. As a group of three, we would definitely have felt like outsiders.

Even if Finley was being a pain in the butt, I had to appreciate the fact that he had brought me here. As if my thoughts conjured him up, he appeared at my elbow. "I assumed you'd have a promise ring on your finger by now," he smirked.

"Has anyone ever told you you're a sick and twisted man?"

He kissed my cheek, catching me totally off guard. "All the time. Now will you dance with me, McKenzie Taylor? I'd like to take a turn around the room with the prettiest girl here."

His flattery was suspect. It made me smile. "I don't know the dances," I said.

"All you have to do is follow me."

"You make it sound so simple." I had my doubts. I'd been known to trip over my own two feet. Yoga classes notwithstanding, I was more stork than flamingo.

"C'mon, lass. Live a little."

I had watched groups of couples doing fairly complicated formations on the floor. This next song, however, was more of a freestyle reel. Finley put one hand at my waist and linked the fingers of his other hand with mine.

"I don't know about this," I muttered.

"Whatever you do, don't stop. 'Twould cause a terrible collision."

The band launched into the song, and we were off. The room spun past me as Finley and I whirled and dipped and moved across the floor. The song was a jig or a reel; I'm not sure I knew the difference. Either way, it was fast. At least a dozen other couples danced with us. I had eyes only for my partner. Flushed and dizzy, I tried to breathe...in between bouts of laughter.

Finley was very popular. Even in the midst of the dance, men shouted out greetings to him. Women gave him the eye. I wondered how many of the local single females had tried to lasso the laconic American. His hand was warm at my waist. I could smell the pleasant tang of his aftershave.

All too soon, it was over. "I loved it," I said impulsively. "How could anyone dance like that and not say goodbye to all their worries?"

Finley tucked a stray hair behind my ear. "Aye. It's wild and sweet and good for the soul. It wasn't really my thing when I first arrived from the States. As I made friends, they bludgeoned me into coming to the ceilidhs. Now, I rarely miss one. Besides, it's intense aerobic training."

I didn't care so much about the physical benefits. All I could think about was how much I had enjoyed being held in Finley's arms. The last hour encompassed everything I hoped I would find in the Scottish Highlands. Tradition. Culture. Art and beauty.

There was only one thing missing.

A proper Scotsman to steal my heart.

Chapter 14

After our crazy dance, we hit the bar. Finley ordered a beer. I asked for water with lime. I was hot and thirsty, and alcohol would only make it worse. Beverages in hand, we made our way to one of the large windows overlooking the street and the harbor. The breeze was perfect—not hot and muggy, not chilly either.

We stood in silence, content to watch the dancers and sip our drinks. I would give a lot to know what Finley was thinking. He was natural with me…comfortable, kind, and attentive. At times, I felt an almost tangible sexual pull between us. I *knew* how I reacted to Finley. Had I imagined his attraction to me?

Troubled by my thoughts, I didn't even notice when the third of Finley's candidates joined us. Finley's voice jerked me out of my reverie.

"McKenzie, I'd like you to meet Allen Gordon."

I turned with a forced smile and felt the breath catch in my throat. The man was taller than Finley, six four at least. He was lean and muscular, and he was wearing an old, clearly well-worn kilt and a white shirt with billowy sleeves. Nine out of ten men in the room wouldn't be able to pull off that style without seeming pretentious. Allen, on the other hand, looked as if he had stepped straight from a movie set…but in a good way.

"Hello, Allen." I stuck out my hand, shooting Finley an incredulous look. I thought Finley was interested in *me*. Why would he trot out this specimen of masculine perfection? Allen's reddish-brown hair and brown eyes gave him a more than passing resemblance to my Outlander crush, Jamie.

My new friend seemed oblivious to any undercurrents. “Finley told me about ye, lass, though he didn’t say how beautiful you are. Reminds me of a young Grace Kelly…am I right, Finley?”

Finley nodded, his face curiously devoid of expression.

Allen took my arm. “This one’s a slow, lovely dance. Will ye have me as your partner, Miss McKenzie?”

“Of course.” I handed Finley my glass and allowed Allen to steer me out onto the dance floor. When he took both of my hands in his and smiled, I was disappointed. I didn’t feel a thing. How was that possible? The man was a gorgeous, redheaded hunk of Scottish beef. I should be dissolving in a puddle of drool about now.

Because this particular reel was slow and lazy, I had no trouble following the various circuits and steps. Allen tossed compliments at me, applauded my dancing and squeezed both of my hands when we were done. “Ye’re a lovely wee lass,” he said as he escorted me back to where my date stood by the window. “This one’s a keeper, Finley. Ye’d better lock her away somewhere before word gets out. Wouldn’t want anyone poaching on your preserves.”

The two men laughed. I wasn’t sure what was so funny. Was Allen making a veiled threat to pursue me? If so, I was flattered, but nothing beyond that. I was far more interested in Finley.

When Allen made his goodbyes and walked away, I turned to Finley, tugged at his shoulder, and whispered in his ear. “No more. I can’t take it. I’m an introvert by nature. Did you know that? Please don’t force me to make nice with anymore of your friends.”

Finley gazed across the crowded room, his expression pensive. “I thought that was the point of your trip. And of tonight, for that matter. Didn’t you come to Scotland to meet your own Jamie Fraser?”

“I suppose.” Hayley and Willow and I had certainly discussed the idea ad nauseam.

“Then what’s the problem?”

“I don’t know. I thought it would happen more organically. Not like a set-up. And besides, you deliberately picked men you knew I wouldn’t go for. The overbearing genealogist? The moping widower? Tell me the truth, Finley. You did it on purpose. To make a point.”

He looked at me and raised an eyebrow. “I fail to see how you could disapprove of Allen Gordon. I’ve seen photos of the actor who plays your Jamie Fraser fellow. Allen could be his brother.”

He had me there. It was impossible to miss the resemblance. Allen was enough to make any woman's pulse flutter. "I'll admit I found him extremely attractive, but there was no spark," I said. "So give up. Please."

Finley's lips twitched, and his eyes danced. "Poor McKenzie. It wouldn't have mattered if you *had* felt a spark."

I frowned. "Why not?"

"Allen is gay."

My mouth gaped. "Really?"

"Really."

I gave him the evil eye. "You are a dirty, rotten scoundrel, Finley Craig. Why would you go out of your way to introduce me to three Scotsmen who were all wrong for me?"

I had my back to the wall. Literally. Finley stood with *his* back to the room, isolating me in the corner. He looked down at me with such intensity in his sapphire eyes that I actually felt faint. "Life isn't a romance novel, McKenzie." He growled the words between clenched teeth. "You're an intelligent, adult woman. Someone needed to knock some sense into you before you get in over your head with a loser who has nothing more to offer than a birth certificate and a Scottish accent."

I couldn't decide if I wanted to smack him or kiss him. His furious lecture was patronizing and insulting. The fact that it was flavored with a faint rolling of the Rs only made his righteous indignation more aggravating. The man might not be Scottish by birth, but he sure as heck had made himself at home.

"My life, *my* romantic fantasy," I snapped, trying not to notice the pulse at the base of his throat. His heart must be beating as fast as mine. "Tonight was an unnecessary charade. If you don't want me to know your friends, I get it. Do me the favor of at least being honest."

He bent his head and whispered, his breath warm on my cheek. "Maybe I wanted to show solidarity with all those American men you're dismissing so easily in favor of Scottish chaps." Then he found my lips with his. "Or maybe," he muttered, "maybe I wanted to keep you for myself."

As kisses went, this one was fairly chaste. After all, we were in the midst of a roomful of people. Finley's lips were warm and firm on mine. Soon I was drunk with the sheer pleasure of kissing him back. He wasn't touching me at all except for the joining of our lips. Still, I felt myself being seduced.

In retrospect, I think I knew what this would be like from the first moment I saw him ride up on his fancy bike, all black leather and badass. Finley Craig was sexy man candy…impossible to resist.

I was parched, gasping for air, burning up from the inside out. Despite our position, *someone* was watching, because I heard catcalls and teasing from Finley's friends. Someone yelled, "Get a room."

I didn't even know that saying translated across the pond.

Pulling back, I broke the kiss and put a hand to my mouth. "It's a little early in the relationship for those kinds of decisions, don't you think?"

He expression was disgruntled, all thwarted male. "For kissing?"

"For keeping," I said, referring to his earlier comment.

"True. Lucky for me, you're not going anywhere anytime soon."

I suspected this was a line he used with many women. The man was gorgeous, single, and comfortably well off…or at least it seemed so. His clients probably paid well for Finley's one-of-a-kind motorcycles.

"We came here to dance," I reminded him. "If you're done, we should go. People are staring at us."

He shrugged. "Let them look. I've barely touched you all night, which should probably qualify me for sainthood. You are a stunningly beautiful woman, Duchess."

The nickname to which I was growing accustomed brought me back to his comment about women who were blond and loaded. Did I remind him of someone in his past? Was he living out a fantasy, using me as a stand-in for a relationship that had gone wrong?

The thought left a bad taste in my mouth. The evening, which had bubbled with all the effervescence of fine champagne, went flat.

"I could use a drink," I said, moving past him to escape the bubble of intimacy.

Finley held my arm. "What did I say? One minute you were leaning into me, and the next I'm getting an Arctic vibe."

I wouldn't make a scene. I knew he would release me if I pressed the issue. The problem was I didn't want him to let go. Not really. "I don't think this is the time or place for fooling around. These people know you."

"So?"

"So they're probably thinking about every other woman you've brought to one of these ceilidhs."

Both of his eyebrows shot toward his hairline. A broad smile covered his face, and his eyes sparkled. "You're jealous? I'll take that as a good sign, my haughty little Duchess."

"I'm not jealous," I said, my voice stiff. "You've lived here a decade. You're several years older than me. I assume you've had other relationships."

"Is this where we exchange our sexual histories?" he asked wryly.

I looked into his eyes, searching for the essence of the man. Was I being strung along by a pro? Or did the dark angel really have a thing for me?

"Maybe we should," I said. If we went back to his house right now, I was almost certain we were going to end up in bed. While that thought made my stomach curl in a good way, I was not a naïve babe in the woods. There were things I wanted to know.

As I retrieved my purse and wrap, Finley said goodbye to many of his friends. Clearly he was well liked. Just as clearly, he had been accepted into this small community as one of their own.

We made our way down the narrow staircase and stepped out into the street.

"It's a beautiful night," Finley said. "Are you up for a stroll?"

"That would be nice." We had walked down the big hill for the party. Going back up would be more challenging. I might as well postpone that for a few minutes. My panting and huffing was going to be embarrassing either way.

We made our way over to the water's edge and looked out at the wine-dark sea. "I like it here," I said softly. "I can feel the presence of the past so clearly. Not in a creepy way. But as though I'm standing on one side of a veil and those other centuries are just beyond my fingertips."

"Forget photography," Finley said. "You should be a poet." He leaned his forearms on the railing, his profile painted by moonlight. He was a beautiful man. I sensed a darkness in him, and that darkness made me cautious.

After a few moments, we found a wooden bench and sat down. Even though I hadn't worn stilettos, my feet hurt from all the jigs and reels. I slipped off my flats and wiggled my toes.

The night wrapped us in promise. I felt a flutter of anticipation in my chest. This trip wasn't turning out as I had expected, but when was life ever predictable? I could enjoy Finley without getting my heart broken. I was a big girl.

He tapped my knee. "Give me your feet," he said. "I'll rub them."

"I won't turn down an offer like that. What do you get in exchange?"

His quick grin was a flash of white in the gloom. "Answers. Tell me your life story, Duchess. Warts and all."

"Very well." I paused, stifling a moan as his thumb dug into the arch of my foot. Damn, the man was good. I'd never had any kind of a foot fetish before today. Apparently, Finley was going to expand my horizons in more ways than one. "I'm an only child," I said. "Willow and Hayley and I have that in common. We're more like sisters than mere friends. I can't imagine my life without them."

"Go on."

Now he was manipulating each individual toe. *Sweet heaven.* I managed not to shudder and moan. It was a close call. "My father owns a huge import-export business based in Atlanta and New York. I grew up mostly in Georgia, but I'm very comfortable in the Big Apple as well."

"And your mother?"

"Social climber. Narcissist. I love her and vice versa. I've often wondered if she gave birth to me only because it was the thing to do. Both of my parents mostly went their own way as I was growing up. The only time they interfered in my life was if I let my grades drop or I hung around with kids they considered socially inferior."

"Willow and Hayley?"

"Yes, for starters. But I lost touch with Willow and Hayley for a decade or more. It wasn't until I finished college that we reconnected and resurrected our friendship."

"Carefully cemented by the glue that is Jamie Fraser."

"Not in the beginning. That came later. Mock all you want. You should read the books. They're extraordinarily well written, and the stories are more than romance if that's what you're thinking."

"You make a very passionate ambassador. Maybe I'll give this Outlander thing a try."

Chapter 15

I felt myself melting into a puddle of yearning. What he was doing to my feet should be illegal. Clearing my throat, I sat up abruptly. "They're better now. Thanks." I put on my shoes like a knight donning armor. I needed to keep some kind of distance between Finley and me at the moment, and with him massaging my feet so erotically, that wasn't going to happen.

He tucked his hands behind his neck and stretched. "I've got a good picture of your childhood. Now let's hear about the men in your life."

"You might not believe me," I said ruefully, "but there haven't been all that many. I went to an all-girls high school and an all-girls college."

"Maybe so, but in college you were away from home, right?"

"Yes." This next part was humiliating. I wasn't sure I wanted to share it, but I could hardly expect Finley to bare his soul if I weren't going to be honest with him. "My first time was with my English professor. Sophomore year." I realized that my hands were clenched in my lap. To move them would only draw attention to how tense I was. I'm not sure what I expected Finley to say, but he surprised me.

He turned to me and smoothed the hair away from my face, rubbing his thumb over my bottom lip. "I get the picture, Duchess. No need to open old wounds. The guy was a bastard."

I thought back to those exhilarating days. I'd been head over heels in lust with the man who spoke so eloquently of Shakespeare and poets and the power of words. In the end, I'd found out the hard way that he was no more than a middle-aged man trying to prove to himself he was still young. Unfortunately, I was not the only naïve girl he'd taken under his wing.

I shook my head, feeling the sting of regret. "Suffice it to say that I waited a long time until I was ready to trust a man again. The end of grad school to be exact. I thought I was finally on the way to getting engaged and living happily ever after. Turns out, though, bachelor number two was far more interested in spending my trust fund than he was in loving me. When I found out and broke up with him, he said I was immature and socially awkward, and that no man would ever see past the money."

The silence fell and gathered weight. I'm not sure why I'd been so detailed in the telling. I could have glossed over it. Maybe it had been too long since I saw my therapist. I wanted to laugh at my own dark humor, but I restrained myself.

Finley reached out and took my right hand in his left. "At the risk of beating a dead horse, is that it?"

"I've dated in the interim, nothing serious."

He massaged my palm with his talented thumb. The man clearly liked to work with his hands. Maybe that's why his motorcycles gave him so much joy.

"Ah, Duchess," he said. "What I wouldn't give to have those two guys alone in a locked room for half an hour."

"Would you beat the crap out of them?" I asked the question with relish.

He chuckled. "I'd sure as hell try. What morons."

"Yeah. I figured that out eventually. The money thing was a bigger millstone than I had realized. People always want something. Good things sometimes. Still, it's hard to feel like an ATM. That's why my two friends who came to Scotland with me are so important. They knew me back before I was a debutante with money. I was just another toddler sharing a Little Tykes tricycle."

"And you didn't go to school together?"

"Only for a few years. My parents decided I needed to be sheltered from the 'bad influences' in public school, so they moved me. Willow ended up leaving, too, for different reasons. When we found each other again, it was as if those years in between never happened."

"You're lucky."

"Yes, I am. Your turn," I said, squeezing his hand.

When he hesitated, I grimaced, even though he couldn't see my face. "I know you've had way more experience than me. Heck, some of the nuns at my high school probably had more experience than me. I don't need a listing, Finley. You could hit the high spots. Particularly concerning a woman who was blond, gorgeous, and loaded. You've left that comment dangling."

His laugh sounded forced. "I knew I never should have mentioned it."

"Do I really remind you of her?" I sensed his ambivalence, though I didn't understand it. Unless he was in love with the woman who got away.

Finley pounded a fist on his knee. "I'm sorry I said it. It's not really true…at least not past a superficial resemblance. Vanessa was greedy and self-centered and high maintenance."

"Ouch. If she was such an ogre, why did you fall in love with her?"

"It's a long story," he warned.

"I can stay up past my bedtime. Honestly."

This time his laugh was the real thing. "Okay. You asked for it. You remember all that stuff about me buckling down in college?"

"Yes."

"Well, it's true. I did. Graduated university with honors and whizzed through a wretchedly difficult MBA. I thought I deserved a pat on the back for that. My dad had other ideas."

"Go on."

"My plan was to take a year off and hitchhike my way through Europe. Decide what I wanted to do with my life. Find myself. All that jazz. Unfortunately, my father had waited long enough for me to shape up and grow up. He wanted me to step into the family business sooner than later."

"And that business is…?"

"My great-grandparents opened one of the first furniture manufacturing companies in North Carolina. They stayed on top decade after decade. My father happily picked up the reins when it was his turn."

"But not you."

"It looked like a prison sentence to me. I tried to talk to my dad. He was having none of it. So he went behind my back and devised plan two."

"How Machiavellian."

"You don't know the half of it. He and another of the big companies saw financial difficulties looming in the distance. They decided that consolidating would give them both an unbreachable stronghold in the area. And they were right. It wasn't enough to agree. Both men thought the deal was only as good as the personal investment."

"I don't understand."

"The other guy had a daughter my age."

"A blond, beautiful daughter."

"You got it. Vanessa was wealthy in her own right, but there was never enough as far as she was concerned. My father hatched a plan for the two of us to meet and offered her fifty thousand dollars if she could get me to commit to her. Daddy dearest knew I'd end up tied to the woman *and* the business, and he would have achieved the endgame."

"You weren't suspicious?"

"I was twenty-four years old and horny from morning to night. Fate drops a gorgeous blonde in my lap. What was I supposed to do? She laughed at all my jokes, offered sex with no strings attached, and did her best to make me fall in love with her."

I was hanging on Finley's every word. I couldn't imagine him being manipulated by anyone, much less a woman. "Did you? Fall in love, I mean?"

"I fell in lust. I'm not sure I knew what love was. The scary thing is, it would have worked if I hadn't stumbled onto the money trail. My father kept his checkbook in the middle drawer of his desk at home. One afternoon I was looking for a paperclip. A damned paperclip. The check register was open, and there was her name and the amount. When I confronted him, he didn't deny it. He said I was too arrogant and stupid to know what was good for me."

"Oh, Finley."

"We had a monstrous shouting match that stopped just short of me bashing his head with a fireplace poker. Bella came in during the middle of it and burst into tears. I walked out and never went back."

"Never?"

"I had worked all during high school and college. Contrary to my father's belief, I wasn't really irresponsible. I had a nice nest egg saved up. I spent a few nights on a buddy's couch coming up with a plan. A week later, I was on a plane for Europe. And you know the rest."

I sat in silence, trying to absorb everything he had said. "You've never mentioned your mother."

"She died when Bella was three and I was eight."

"Did your father every remarry?"

"Yep. Six months after I left for Europe, he married Vanessa."

The blunt statement stunned me. Finley had been betrayed several times over by the man who should have been firmly in his corner. "Oh, God. That's dreadful."

"Yeah. Needless to say, I didn't go to the wedding. Those were pretty much the most humiliating months of my life. Dear Bella refused to lose contact with me, even though with the mood I was in I wasn't much of a brother."

"I don't understand. You said Bella's getting a doctorate. Didn't your father pressure her into the family business as well?"

"Bella was always brilliant. Everyone knew she was destined for a bright future. Besides, my father is very old fashioned. The whole father-to-son lineage thing is important to him. Very biblical."

"Has Bella *ever* visited you here?"

"A handful of times. After I left home, it was several years until she made it to Skye. At first, my father wouldn't allow it. Then by the time she was on her own, she was neck deep in her studies."

"How often have you been back to the States?"

"Never. I had planned to go home for her college graduation. She begged me not to. She knew Dad and Vanessa would be there, and she didn't want to risk an embarrassing scene."

"Surely she knew you wouldn't ruin her special day."

"Not me. Vanessa. My stepmother is a drama queen in every sense of the word. It's best for everybody if I give my 'parents' a wide berth."

"Did your father marry Vanessa to punish you?" I couldn't imagine such a cold-hearted parent.

"I think she seduced him and not the other way around, although it probably occurred to him that hooking up with my ex would be a way to turn the knife. No, the punishment for my defection was writing me out of his will. As it stands now, Bella will inherit everything. And I'm fine with that."

"She'll probably give you your half when the time comes…won't she?"

"Maybe. I won't take it. She deserves the money for sticking around and putting up with my father."

"I don't even know what to say, Finley. My mom and dad are not exactly shining examples of good parenting, but their style was more benign neglect than outright manipulation. I'm so sorry."

"It was a long time ago. I've moved on."

That was perhaps the first lie Finley Craig had ever told me. He was still deeply hurt, or else his father wouldn't have the emotional power to keep Finley away. A man without a country…that's what Finley was. His self-imposed exile reminded him every day of his youthful mistake.

He was hardly the first man to be fooled by a woman. The experience had been compounded by the fact his father had been complicit in the whole scheme.

We had barely scratched the surface of Finley's past. There were ten years of Scottish history unaccounted for. Suddenly, I wasn't interested in a litany of his relationships while he'd been living in Portree.

I was far more curious about what was going to happen when we went back up the hill.

Chapter 16

"It's late," I said. "I'm starting to get chilled. Do you mind if we go home?"

"Not at all."

He must have realized I wasn't going to press for more details about his love life. Was he glad? Or did he have nothing to hide? It didn't really matter now. It was pretty clear to me that what happened a decade ago had indelibly shaped both his outlook on life and his attitude toward women.

No wonder he had been so prickly with me when I arrived. With my fancy luggage and couture clothes, he had pigeonholed me immediately. He couldn't know that the luggage was a dozen years old or that I kept the same classic items of clothing for several years.

I enjoyed fashion. What woman didn't? Even so, my closet was relatively small. I didn't collect for the sake of collecting. A few good staple pieces and a handful of jewelry were my usual style.

Without speaking, we stood and began the climb up to Finley's house. He had left a few lights burning. Their glow welcomed us in the darkness. I would be sad to leave tomorrow. No matter how comfy Cedric's house became, it would never have the charm of this one, because it wouldn't have Finley and Cinnamon.

I stumbled going up the steps. Finley grabbed for my elbow automatically and steadied me. In the hushed breath of a passing second, I knew what he was thinking. His grip gentled, and he stepped away…even though I would have bet my last twenty pound note that he wanted me.

"Goodnight, McKenzie," he said. "I'll be in shortly and lock up."

He was playing the civilized host, not taking advantage of our situation. While I appreciated his restraint, I was in a more volatile place. "Do you want me in your bed, Finley?" I asked, my heart pounding in my chest.

"Don't be naïve," he snapped. "You know what I want." He paused. "Are you sure?" The question was barely audible.

"Sure enough for now," I said rashly. "This trip to Scotland is supposed to be about enjoying new experiences. I choose you."

"McKenzie…" He said my name in a hushed whisper that made me tremble. "I'd be a fool to say no."

"I have it on good authority that you're a very intelligent man. We don't have to overthink this. I'm spreading my wings. Getting out of a rut. I know what I'm doing, I swear. You don't have to worry I'll be underfoot every time you turn around. That's not my style."

"I wouldn't mind if you were," he said mildly as he ruffled his fingers through my hair.

When his big, warm hands settled on my bare shoulders, something happened to me. I don't know if it was the moon or the dancing or the fact that I was deep in the Scottish Highlands, but I succumbed to some kind of spell. The world fell away bit by bit until all I knew was Finley.

The way he touched me—so hungry and yet so sweet. The sound of his breathing, harsh and ragged. The dampness of the skin at the back of his neck when I caressed the place where his hair met his collar.

My brain shut down, at least the portion that contained reason and logic. All I could do was feel and feel and feel. In my ballet flats, I was small and defenseless. Finley was tall and strong and unmistakably masculine. "Take me inside," I pleaded. *Before I change my mind.* I couldn't even blame my reckless decision on alcohol. I was stone cold sober.

Finley scooped me into his arms. For a man who insisted that life wasn't a romance novel, he damned sure acted like a storybook hero. I rested my cheek against his collarbone and pressed my hand over his heart.

Time lost all meaning. Cradled in Finley's embrace, I was content to drift as he locked the door and carried me upstairs. He bypassed my room and went on to his. Unfortunately, our romantic moment ground to a halt when we heard Cinnamon barking mournfully in the distance.

"Damned dog." Finley sighed.

I knew he didn't mean it. A man in certain situations is hard pressed to focus on anything other than the mission at hand. I kissed his cheek. "Go take her out. I'll wait. It's okay."

Finley set me on my feet and disappeared. In the distance I could hear the interaction between man and dog before they went outside. Given a reprieve to assess the situation, I smiled ruefully. I wasn't going to back out now. This encounter was no adrenaline-fueled decision in the heat of the moment. I knew what I was doing. And I knew the risk I was taking.

Finley Craig was the kind of man who broke hearts.

He was wary. Cynical. Distrustful of women in general.

Unfortunately, he was exactly what I wanted.

I sat on the edge of the bed and tested the mattress with my hand. Finley's bed was as beautiful as the man himself. The wooden frame and headboard were simple and stunning, the oak polished with the sheen of long use. I wondered if it was an antique. The room was almost monastic in its simplicity. A single dresser occupied one wall. A more modern entertainment armoire faced the bed.

The walls were painted the palest of greens, the color of light in a summer forest. The single large window was flanked with raw linen draperies. Everything was perfectly neat. Did the housekeeper work this magic? Or was the complicated man with the painful past in need of a peaceful place to unwind at the end of a long day?

I had assumed Finley would hurry Cinnamon outside and back in again quickly. Perhaps the dog was being contrary. Or maybe Finley was rethinking our rash tumble into bed. It hurt to imagine that some of his caution might be in regard to me. I was rich and blond and moderately attractive. Certainly not gorgeous. My chin was too strong for classical female beauty. And I'd never been thin since I went through puberty.

Still, it was clear that who I was triggered some kind of post-traumatic stress for Finley. I reminded him of a time in his life he'd rather forget.

Chastened and hurting, I paced the floor, barely noticing the loud tick of the clock. I should go back to my room. Cinnamon's presence in the house had saved me from making a bad mistake. Clearly, the time-out had brought Finley to his senses, as well.

It was time for me to go. I had my hand on the door when it opened abruptly, whacking me in the head. "Ouch," I cried, stumbling backward.

Finley gaped at me. "McKenzie. What were you doing?"

I rubbed the red spot on my forehead. "So this is my fault?" I asked crossly.

He picked me up by the waist and set me on the bed. "Let me see."

His thumb feathered across my eyebrow as he examined my injury. "It may bruise. I'm sorry, Duchess."

I shrugged. "It's fine." I couldn't quite look him in the eye. "It's late," I said. "I should get some sleep. I have a big day tomorrow."

He sat down beside me, making the mattress dip and tumbling me against his shoulder. "What's wrong, McKenzie?"

"Nothing. Everything. I don't want to remind you of her." I folded my arms across my chest. "You were gone so long I thought you must have changed your mind."

"About having sex with you?"

I nodded jerkily.

"Look at me," he demanded.

When I reluctantly complied, he turned sideways to face me and held out his hands. "*This* is what took so long."

His long masculine fingers distracted me for a moment. Then I noticed the angry red burn on his right hand. The flesh in the center of his palm was raw. "Oh, Finley. What happened?"

"Cinnamon," he said ruefully. "She heard something in the woods and caught me off guard. I tried to stop her and got a rope burn when she yanked the leash right out of my hand."

"I'm sorry that happened. I was going to my room, because I thought we weren't going to…well, you know."

His gentle smile was quizzical. "No. That's not it at all. I had to catch up with my wretched dog, drag her back to the house, and put her away for the night. Then I had to clean my hand. I never meant to leave you for so long."

This was as good a time as any to call a halt before we did something that might look very different in the cold light of morning. I took a deep breath. "I don't want to have sex with you because I remind you of Vanessa."

Finley didn't react at first. In fact, if I hadn't been studying him so closely, I might not even have seen the barest flicker of his eyelashes. "Why would you think that?"

"She's a myth. Somebody frozen in the past. No matter who she *really* is, you have this painful, decade-old memory of her."

His jaw turned to granite. A look I was beginning to understand was his reaction to anyone who pissed him off or dared to enter emotional rooms labeled *hands off.*

The muscles in his throat worked. "I don't need a shrink, Duchess. And even if I did, you're not exactly qualified."

His chilly tone gave me goose bumps. I'd always believed that heated confrontations were healthier than icy ones. Sometimes his blue eyes glowed with fire and life. Now, they were cold enough to shatter.

Near tears, I pressed on, knowing even as I did so that I was going to regret my honesty. “You’re welcome to hide out here in Scotland until you’re a shriveled-up old man,” I said. “Despite the chemistry you and I have between us, I won’t be a stand-in for another woman, no matter what your twisted reasons for making love to me.”

“*Fucking*,” he said. “It’s called fucking. Don’t paint this as some kind of romantic fantasy.”

I stared at him, incredulous that the charming man I knew could be so deliberately cruel. Shaking all over, I stood up on legs the consistency of spaghetti. All I wanted to do was make it out of the room without collapsing. “I appreciate your honesty,” I said, my throat raw. “I doubt we’ll see each other again, so I’ll say goodbye. Thank you for the roadside rescue and for the room and board.”

I waited for him to stop me. To tell me he was sorry. To erase the hurtful words with soft kisses.

But he didn’t.

He let me walk out of his bedroom and close the door behind me.

When I got to my own room, I locked the door and stripped off my clothes. I was so cold I didn’t think I’d ever be warm again. In the tiny bathroom, I started the shower and ran it as hot as I could bear it.

Then I stepped into the tub so no one would hear me sob.

I cried because I missed my friends and for the aching emptiness inside me and because Finley had tarnished my dream of Scotland. The trip of a lifetime had been reduced to a date-night gone bad. One more in a line of sad stories about men who weren’t worth my time or my emotional investment.

The trouble was, crying never solved anything. In the end, it left you with a stuffy nose and a hollow certainty that few things in life lived up to the hype. Perhaps I was becoming as cynical as my host.

I found my comfiest pajamas and pulled on fluffy woolen socks. My feet were numb. Despite the hot shower, I still felt cold to the bone. After climbing into the big bed, I huddled under the covers, flung an arm across my face, and listened to myself breathe.

How could I have such a pain in my chest? It’s not as if Finley Craig was the love of my life. Even so, my pillowcase was damp when I finally managed to fall asleep.

Chapter 17

The next morning, I awoke to gray skies. I didn't even care. The weather matched my mood. Suddenly, I was desperate to escape from Finley's house without seeing him again.

I needn't have worried. The man was nowhere to be found. I packed up my things haphazardly. I wasn't going far. Part of me needed to make a big dramatic gesture and throw the black dress with the rhinestone clasp into the trash. Not only was it the single really dressy thing I'd brought with me on the trip, I didn't want to give Finley the idea I was upset.

Let him think our time together was nothing more than a blip on my radar. He was nothing to me. Nothing at all. I cared more about his sweet, mischievous dog than I did about a closed off, emotionally stunted alpha male.

Sadly, even Cinnamon deserted me…no opportunity for goodbyes on that front either. She was probably in the workshop with her master. The same workshop that was off limits to me.

When I was ready, I took one last look at the room where I had spent my first nights on the Isle of Skye. I'd been careful to erase every evidence of my stay in Finley's home. I felt as if I had lived a lifetime since my car went into a ditch. Certainly not what I had expected. Then again, life rarely went according to plan.

I fell into a weird sort of emotionless calm as I loaded the car and drove away. I was almost positive Finley was around somewhere. Clearly, he had no desire to bump into me. I wouldn't let his indifference hurt me.

The drive to my new lodgings took longer than it should have. The rain had set in. I managed to find a radio station with a weather report. Apparently, the Scottish Highlands were being buffeted with the remains of Hurricane Mabel. It had made its way across the Atlantic, losing its hurricane-strength winds, but still powerful enough to stall out and dump almost unprecedented amounts of rain.

Mrs. Clark had hidden the house key under a rock. Hunched over beneath an umbrella that was barely able to keep the worst of the rain off my neck, I found the key and let myself in.

I'd prepared for disappointment. It was a raw, gloomy day, and the house would probably be damp and unwelcoming. I had underestimated the sturdy Scottish cleaning lady. As soon as I opened the front door and shrugged out of my wet rain jacket, the smell of lemon furniture polish surrounded me.

Even a cursory inspection told me the house had been totally overhauled. I was so grateful I wanted to sit down and weep. Instead, I wiped my nose, put my coat back on, and unloaded the car. It didn't make any sense to wait. There would be no break in the weather anytime soon.

At her insistence, Mrs. Clark had also stocked the fridge and cabinets with staples. Even if the storm lasted several days, I wouldn't starve. Soup and sandwiches, if nothing else, would sustain me.

I picked the larger of the two bedrooms and unpacked my bags and carry-on, putting things away in a rickety bureau and hanging a few items in the alcove that passed for a closet. Then I went back into the main room and put a match to the pile of kindling in the fireplace. Soon the smell of wood smoke mingled with the lemon scent.

After boiling a pot of water and brewing myself a cup of tea, I pulled a rocking chair close to the hearth and warmed my toes as I sipped my drink. I wondered what Hayley and Willow were up to. Had the rain impacted their plans? Though neither of my friends was all that far from me as the crow flies, I felt a million miles from them *and* from civilization. Here I was, tucked away in my pleasantly secluded rental house, and all I could think about was the faux Scotsman with brilliant blue eyes and a tendency to be a curmudgeon.

Dogs were good judges of character. If Cinnamon loved Finley, I should give the man the benefit of the doubt. We had let our hormones run away with us, and we had shared too much personal information too soon.

When I looked past my own hurt and disappointment, I couldn't really fault Finley for speaking the blunt truth. I'd spun him a tale of three women crossing the ocean in search of adventure and romance fueled by a novel of time travel. It must have sounded far-fetched to say the least. I suppose it made sense that he didn't want to give me the wrong idea.

At noon I opened the package of crusty bread and cobbled together a messy grilled cheese sandwich. Along with a cup of cocoa, the comfort food made me feel a little less hollow inside.

After reading for an hour, I found myself on my feet pacing the confines of the modest house. I'd fantasized for weeks about what it would be like to be alone with my thoughts…to have the freedom to do anything or nothing. In my dreams, though, I'd been ranging around the Scottish hillsides, soaking up the summer sun, and taking photos to my heart's content.

It appeared that my camera was going to sit idle for quite some time. Unless of course I wanted to do still life portraits of ordinary fruit and artsy shots of raindrops on windowpanes.

Though it was pointless, I checked my cell phone again. No bars at all. I wasn't going to be able to check in with Hayley and Willow every night at nine. I knew they were grown women and very competent women at that. Being cut off was an odd and worrisome feeling in this day of über-connectedness.

At least I had the landline. Though it seemed old-fashioned at best, the phone with the rotary dial was all that stood between me and complete isolation. That was a completely reassuring backup until midafternoon when I lifted the receiver and realized the phone lines were out of commission.

My imagination went haywire suddenly. What if my appendix burst? What if I cut my hand with a kitchen knife? What if a spark from the fireplace set the whole cottage ablaze?

In the end, none of it mattered. I was essentially helpless to change my situation in the short term. Unless I was prepared to make my way back to Portree and sleep in my car, this small house was my only shelter from the storm.

The hours passed with agonizing slowness. By late afternoon, the skies had darkened to the point it seemed almost like night. The rain thundered now, the roar a steady, menacing presence. I was usually a fan of rainy days. This was something else again.

When I peered out the front window, I could barely see my rental car. It seemed as if a river of mud surrounded the vehicle. I couldn't be sure, and I definitely wasn't going outside to check.

Dinner was a reprise of lunch. Only this time I opened a can of tomato soup and heated it to go along with the sandwich. Mrs. Clark had left a bouquet of wildflowers in a clear glass jar in the center of the kitchen table. The cheery yellow blossoms kept me company while I ate.

For someone who had logged many weeks and months as a world traveler, I had woefully underestimated my tolerance for solitude. It honestly never occurred to me that I could be trapped inside. I knew it was often cloudy and gray in Scotland, but a tropical storm? That twist seemed far-fetched.

Yet here I was…a victim of my own careful planning.

The little cottage creaked and groaned beneath the force of the wind and the rain. So far, no leaks in the roof. I didn't know how long that would last. Cedric's home was at least half a mile up the hillside. The rest of the small mountain loomed above me, obscured by the storm.

By eight o'clock I had drunk so many cups of tea I knew I was destined for a sleepless night. Still, tea or no tea, the storm would no doubt keep me awake. I took a shower and changed into the same cotton pajamas that had comforted me last night.

It was hard to believe that only twenty-four hours had passed since Finley and I quarreled. Already, the episode seemed a lifetime ago. What was fresh and real, however, was the memory of how he had carried me into the house en route to our night of passion.

I knew the term *coitus interruptus*. Unfortunately, there was no good description for what had happened to Finley and me. We'd never gotten past the first kiss. Thanks to Cinnamon's antics, I would never know if intimacy with Finley Craig was actually as thrilling as the anticipation.

I stood at the window beside the front door, my palm pressed to the glass. Cabin fever set in with a vengeance, along with a healthy dose of paranoia.

It occurred to me in the midst of my mental gymnastics that I was well on my way to an old-fashioned fit of the vapors. There was no one around to see me have a meltdown, so why did it matter?

Since it was far too early to go to bed, I perused Cedric's single bookshelf for something to read. I had my Kindle, but I wanted to preserve the battery for emergencies.

The choices in my current abode were limited. The Bible. A Scottish version of the farmer's almanac. Several lurid crime novels. *No, thank you*. And last, but not least, five or six volumes of folktales.

At least, that's what I called them. I guess if you were an old man from Scotland—like Cedric—they were simply stories.

I picked up the fattest of the lot and reclaimed my rocking chair. Though in the beginning, I had to force myself to absorb the words on the page, soon I was drawn into a world of fairies and witches and changelings and pagan dances under the harvest moon.

The Gaelic heritage came with a healthy dose of superstition and whimsy. Some of the stories made me smile. Others sent a shiver down my spine. My favorite was a tale so skillfully crafted, I found myself wanting it to be true. It was about a farm lad spirited away every night by a witch who put a magic bridle around his head and turned him into a horse.

The crafty witch forced him to gallop across the moors until he was dead exhausted. Then she led him home to his farmhouse, took off the bridle, and tucked him back into bed. Every morning the poor lad was gaunter and more ill than the day before. The boy's brother began to suspect magic afoot. So one night he slept in the brother's bed and let the witch take him.

The same sequence of events occurred, but when the witch stopped by the farmhouse of one of her evil acquaintances, she put the horse in a stall in the barn. The wily brother in horse form chewed off his own bridle and was changed back into a man. He slipped into the house and killed the witch and her cohorts. Only then did the other brother begin to recover from his mysterious illness.

I closed the book and stared into the fire, trying to imagine a time when every inexplicable twist and turn in life was explained by the work of unseen creatures, malevolent ones at that. No electricity. No hospitals. No instant communication with everyone else in a person's life.

The entire world likely consisted of a few square miles where a man or woman was born, lived, and died. The book slipped from my lap. I let it fall, stricken by the knowledge that I had come to Scotland in search of a life that wasn't even my own. I wanted to be someone else. Not the heiress. Not the dutiful daughter. Not even the friend who paid for an expensive trip.

I was thirty-two years old, and I had no idea who I was or who I wanted to be. What kind of messed up head-game was I playing with myself? Photography? A lonely house in the middle of nowhere? What did I expect to find on the Isle of Skye? A personal rebirth? A miracle?

The fire had burned down to nothing while I sat and rocked. I felt empty inside. Numb. Somehow, Finley had seen the truth and called me on my bullshit. Somehow he knew that my quest for adventure and my own Jamie Fraser was a cover for the fact that I had no idea *what* I wanted.

My whole life up until this point had been scripted for me. Even though I had moved out of my parents' shadow long ago, I had never quite found my niche. Part society belle, part modern philanthropist, I was a walking, talking cliché.

Chapter 18

For a long moment I wondered if some force within the walls of this small, nondescript house had bewitched me. McKenzie Taylor was smart, focused, and confident. At least that's what the world thought…what my friends thought.

I'd learned long ago not to reveal my weaknesses. Hayley and Willow believed I had chosen this self-catering cottage because I didn't like hotels. That was partly true, I suppose. I did like my privacy.

Now, in the midst of an unlikely tropical storm on the Scottish moors, I would give my last dollar to be tucked into the nearest Holiday Inn Express with matchy-matchy art on the walls and plenty of vending machines.

I jumped six inches when a loud pounding at the door startled me out of my mental epiphany. Hurrying across the room, I peeked out the window to see a tall man who bore a striking resemblance to Finley. Behind him a black Jeep sat at a drunken angle. In his arms he held a large blob wrapped in a blanket. A black backpack was slung over his shoulder.

He saw my face and motioned. "Let me in!"

I fumbled with the latch twice before my trembling fingers conquered the mechanism and the door swung wide. The rain was coming sideways now. I jumped back as Finley lurched over the doorstep and stumbled inside, dropping his blanketed load in the process.

With a bark and violent shaking, Cinnamon expressed her disapproval for the indignity to which she'd been subjected. I knelt beside her. "Poor baby. You're wet and cold."

Finley wiped a hand across his face. "I wouldn't get too close if I were you," he warned. "She got away from me when I tried to put her in the

Jeep and now she's muddy. I wiped off what I could, but she's not exactly fit to be inside."

"It doesn't matter. Let me get the fire going again, and she can sit by the hearth to dry out."

"Do I merit the same offer?" He smiled, though the smile didn't reach his eyes.

My pajamas were thin. My robe was in the bedroom. With my hair tied up in a scraggly knot on top of my head, I found myself at a distinct disadvantage. Finley might be wet and windblown, but at least *he* was fully clothed.

I folded my arms across my breasts. "What are you doing here, Finley?"

He shrugged out of his heavy rain slicker and hung it on a peg beside the door. "I was worried about you. The roads are virtually impassable now, and the authorities are issuing warnings about landslides."

I understood what he meant. Much of the landscape was not forested. The green hills had little in the way of root systems to keep the earth in place under conditions like these.

"As you can see, I'm fine. You shouldn't linger if it's that bad. You and Cinnamon need to get back to town while you still can."

I was proud of my speech. Even in pajamas, I gave him my best *I'm-in-control* imitation. The fact that my words were all a pile of pooh was irrelevant.

Luckily for me, Finley ignored my posturing. He squatted in front of the fireplace and began stacking wood with economical movements that told me he knew what he was doing. Soon the crackling and popping of a roaring blaze filled the room with sound and color and warmth.

Poor Cinnamon must have worn herself out earlier. She was already asleep, curled up with her tail wrapped around her nose. The wretched dog had abandoned me. I could have used a distraction.

"I'm serious, Finley," I said. "You need to go if it's that bad."

He stood and wiped his hands on his pant legs. "I'm not leaving you here alone."

Well. What was I supposed to say to that?

When I stood there, mute, he came to me and put his hands on my shoulders. "I'm sorry, Duchess." He kissed my forehead. "I did want to make love to you last night, but when you brought up Vanessa, it made me angry."

I slipped my arms around his waist and let him hold me closer. "I know. I was wrong to mention it."

His big frame tensed. If he still felt this much emotion for the woman who had betrayed him, I'd be a fool to get involved.

He shook his head. A mighty sigh rumbled through his chest. I felt the steady *ka-thud* of his heartbeat, more rapid than it should have been.

"You've misunderstood, McKenzie. I didn't want to make love to you *because* you reminded me of Vanessa. I wanted you *in spite of* the physical resemblance. There's a big difference."

I flinched inwardly. Did Finley have a type? Being linked in any way with the woman who had been so manipulative of son and father made me uncomfortable. "I understand." *I think.*

Though staying in Finley's embrace would be a lovely antidote to the day's solitude, I eluded his embrace. Physically. Mentally. "I was almost ready to go to bed when you arrived," I said. "Thanks to Mrs. Clark, the guest room is ready. Make yourself at home. Do you really think we're in any danger here?"

As a change of subject, it was clumsy. Finley gave me my space. He shrugged. "Cedric's cottage has been on this mountainside for decades. So probably not. Though I never underestimate Mother Nature." He grimaced. "I don't suppose you have any decaf, do you?"

"Sorry. No coffee at all. I could make you some herbal tea." Even as the words left my mouth I had to laugh. "You're not exactly the herbal tea type, are you?"

He cocked his head and stared at me with those deep blue eyes. "I could be persuaded. If you promise to join me."

I chewed my bottom lip. "We need to back up a few steps," I said quietly. "Last night told me that neither one of us is ready to…well, you know…"

He winced. "I'm sorry I said what I did. I was being a jackass. Maybe I do have some old baggage to sort through. It has nothing to do with you."

"I believe you, Finley. I do. Let's hit the restart button. Okay?"

"Fair enough. I'd still like that drink."

While I measured out the loose tea leaves and found matching pottery mugs in the cabinet, Finley pulled the second rocking chair by the fire adjacent to mine. Nothing was going to happen tonight. Why was I still as jittery as a teenager en route to the prom?

I added one sugar to my cup and three to his. The man had a sweet tooth. I'd noticed as much in the brief course of our acquaintance. When I handed him his tea, he wrapped his fingers around the warm crockery and sat down with a sigh.

"How are things in Portree?" I asked, joining him by the fire.

"My place is fine. Unfortunately, there's already flood damage in town, and it will only get worse."

"But we're on an island. The ocean doesn't flood."

"No. You've seen the way the town sits, though. It's a funnel. The rain is falling so hard, so fast, that as it rushes down from the higher ground, it's creating rivers or waterfalls, whatever you want to call it. We'll have a lot of cleanup ahead."

I knew the word *we* didn't include me. Finley was a permanent resident of Portree, part of the town. He would pitch in with his fellow citizens to do what had to be done. I envied him in many ways. I'd never had an opportunity to try the small-town lifestyle. It seemed charming and peaceful, but would I enjoy it long term?

Finley finished his drink and set his cup on the floor. Then he ran both hands through his hair and sighed. "I don't know what it is about you, Duchess. I feel as if I've known you a lot longer than I really have."

I nodded slowly. "Maybe it's because I'm someone from home, and we have a background in common."

"I don't think so." He stood and poked the fire, then straightened and rested one arm on the mantel. In profile, his features were strong and masculine. I could imagine a Renaissance artist wanting to paint or sculpt him.

"Does Scotland really feel like home to you?" I asked.

He grimaced. "In some ways."

"But not all."

"No."

"Do you ever plan to go back? For good, I mean?"

He crouched suddenly in front of my rocker, his hand on my knees. "You ask a hell of a lot of questions, Duchess."

"Sorry." I wasn't really. It seemed like the thing to say. From this angle, I could see a silver thread here and there in his dark, glossy hair. Finley was no callow youth. He was a man. And he carried with him a man's hurts.

I touched his cheek tentatively, almost expecting him to bat my hand away. "I'm not a spoiled heiress, Finley. At least I don't think I am."

His grin lit a spark in my belly. "I'm pretty clear on that now."

"What do you mean?"

"I googled you last night. Why didn't you tell me?"

"Tell you what?"

"That you've singlehandedly done all the interior design work for every Habitat for Humanity house that's been built in the state of Georgia for the last four years." His grin faded, replaced by a sober regard that made me antsy.

He had me boxed in, physically. I stood up abruptly and escaped to the other side of the room, tidying things at the sink. "It's no big deal. It's a way to use my training, and I don't need to get paid for the work. So it's a win-win for everyone."

"Ah, Duchess." He followed me easily. There wasn't much room for retreat in this tiny house.

When his arms came around me from behind, I stiffened. I wanted this too badly to botch things a second time. "What are you doing?" I asked.

"Hugging you?"

"Doesn't that seem kind of personal?"

"You don't like hugs?"

Come to think of it, I didn't. Except with Willow and Hayley, I wasn't very good at physical affection. Even now, my heart raced and my forehead was damp. Finley surrounded me with his presence…his scent, his touch. I felt him tall and warm at my back. His strong arms held me firmly. I knew I could break free if I wanted to. That wasn't the problem.

My dilemma was wanting so much more. Calmly, I dried my hands on a dishtowel and turned around. "Hugs are okay," I said, searching his eyes for the answers to questions I hadn't even asked yet. "I think with you I prefer them this way."

I pressed a fingertip to the center of his bottom lip. When he trembled, I was torn between astonishment and euphoria. He wanted me.

He swallowed hard, his Adam's apple moving noticeably. "Whatcha doin' there, Duchess?"

It had been a very long time since I felt such a rush of sexual hunger. I wanted to gobble him up. "We may be trapped here forever," I said softly. "Wouldn't that be terrible?"

He kissed my nose. "Awful, Duchess. Impossible, maybe."

"People in times of crisis have to survive the best they can."

"True." He shuddered when I nipped his chin with my teeth.

I was playing a game that wasn't fair to either of us. "Tell me to stop," I said breathlessly.

He bit my earlobe. "Stop."

"That was about the most unconvincing command I've ever heard." Was I using Finley because I was scared to be alone? Or did this odd and unexpected connection have a future?

His voice came out muffled because he was kissing every inch of my neck. Only the collar of my pajama top stopped him. “I’m sorry for what I said yesterday,” he groaned. “Forgive me, Duchess.”

“You’ve already apologized,” I pointed out, though I couldn’t help being gratified by his groveling.

“I need you to know I mean it. When I take you to bed it won’t be what I said.”

“Fucking?”

He put his hand over my mouth, clearly not amused. “I said I was sorry. I want to make love to you, McKenzie. But not tonight. I need you to know that when it does happen it means something more to me than a quick roll in the hay. So while we’re stuck here with each other, let’s see how far we can get.”

Chapter 19

He charmed and disarmed me. I cocked my head. "Are we dating, Finley? Is that it?"

"Under the circumstances, I think 'dating' is the least of what we're doing."

"We could have a slumber party in front of the fire."

I saw him go still. "Are you serious?"

"Why not? We'd have Cinnamon as a chaperone. And this room is so warm and cozy now, those two bedrooms are not at all appealing."

His slow, lazy smile made my toes curl in my wooly socks. "I like a woman with a plan."

"What if I go brush my teeth while you drag the mattresses in here? Then after that, the bathroom will be all yours."

"Works for me."

When I watched him leave the room, I exhaled a big whoosh of air. I was playing with fire, no doubt about it. Ruefully, I thought of all the beautiful nightwear I owned back in my condo in Atlanta. I loved feminine silks and satins and lace. For Scotland, though, I had chosen practical over pretty.

Oh, well. He'd already seen me now in my unexciting pj's. At least I could brush my hair and add a spritz of scent at my wrists and anywhere else it might be discovered.

In the bathroom, I stared at my reflection in the mirror over the sink. The glass was old and mottled, with a crack across the top left corner. "What are you doing McKenzie? Be smart about this."

I often gave myself pep talks before important occasions. Seldom, though, did I have such an urgent need to throw caution to the wind.

Ten minutes was more than enough time to take care of my bedtime routine. I stayed an extra five, for no other reason than to see if I could stop shaking. It worked. Mostly.

When I returned to the other room, I gaped. Finley had made quick work of his assigned task. He'd situated both mattresses in front of the fire so that our feet would stay toasty warm. He had transferred all the sheets and blankets and tucked them neatly in place. The only thing that surprised me was the four-foot no-man's-land between the two mattresses.

He gave me a terse nod and disappeared into the bathroom with his backpack.

I knew I didn't have long to make a decision. Did I want to keep boundaries in place, or did I want to fool around with Finley?

In the end, I chickened out. I left the mattresses as they were.

When Finley reappeared, he grimaced. "I have to take the dog out. We'll be quick." He reached for his rain slicker, put it on, and pulled up the hood.

For once, Cinnamon was not visibly eager to explore the outdoors. She went with Finley, but they were back in no time, both of them soaked and miserable. Finley used the old blanket to dry the dog. Cinnamon reclaimed her spot on the hearth while Finley shook water droplets from his coat and put it back on the peg by the door.

At last, he approached the fireplace. I had claimed the mattress on the left. He removed his shoes, took off his belt, and crouched to slide under the covers.

I turned on my side to face him. "How long have you had her? The dog, I mean."

Finley yawned and stretched. "A year and a half. She was six weeks old when I bought her." He turned to face me. "Do you really want to talk about my dog?"

His blue eyes were shadowed. I had turned off all the lights, so our only illumination was from the fire. I studied his face, trying to decide what it was about him that drew me so strongly. He was an interesting contradiction: part artist, part entrepreneur. Unflinchingly masculine.

His sexual appeal was overt. I'd seen more than one woman at the dance last night giving him the eye. Though he was friendly and charming, he carried himself with reserve. I wondered if anyone in Portree knew the real Finley.

"Maybe you should ask *me* questions," I said, conceding defeat. He would tell me only as much as he was willing to tell, no matter how many times I pressed him.

He mimicked my position, sprawling on his left side to face me. "I suppose this is old hat to you…slumber parties and all."

"My first one," I said simply.

"You're kidding." His eyebrows shot to his hairline.

"It was the whole 'mingling with riffraff thing,' remember? Slumber parties were far too bourgeois for my parents. They'd send me on supervised play dates at the Met in New York. Or enroll me in continuing ed classes at Emory in Atlanta. Free time was not a highly valued commodity in our household, especially not free time that involved playmates who weren't 'our kind of people.'"

"So how did you escape growing up as an unbearable prima donna?"

"I probably was as a kid," I said honestly. "Fortunately, when I made it to high school, our curriculum included modules of volunteer work in the community. Those classes were a requirement, so my parents couldn't quibble over it. Seeing how the other half lived shocked me and made me a better person, I hope."

Finley's gaze was drowsy, his eyelids heavy. Sexual tension lingered just off stage, but we were both tired. Added to that was the ever-present noise of the storm. "I didn't expect this," he said.

I searched his face, confused. "Spending the night here?"

"I didn't expect *you.*" The words were flat and not altogether flattering.

My insides curled into a tight wad of hurt. "The rain will be over sometime, Finley. After that you won't have to worry about me anymore."

Why did relationships have to be so messy? Finley's past was an emotional wreck. Mine was less dramatic but equally disheartening. Wasn't love supposed to be easy and fun? I knew dozens of girls in college who slept their way through entire rugby teams and never gave it a second thought.

Yet here I was, drawn to a gorgeous, moody, complicated man and quite unable to tell him I wanted a vacation fling.

Maybe that was the problem. I wanted more, and it was hard to lie convincingly even to myself.

I saw his eyes close, so I swallowed my disappointment. It was for the best. This entire situation was artificial. The secluded house. The violent storm. The proximity that neither of us had engineered deliberately. I had belatedly kept to my travel itinerary, and Finley was simply being conscientious about looking out for a friend.

Sighing quietly, I let sleep drag at my limbs. Having Finley nearby, no matter our emotional state, was reassuring on a visceral level. He might inadvertently break my heart, but I would come to no physical harm as long as he was with me.

I dozed after that, fitfully and restlessly. Between those rare moments when I slept deeply, I was aware of Finley rising to add wood to the fire and of him peering out the window by the door, his back to me as he stared out into the black night.

Sometime after four, a thunderous crash jerked us awake. I know I cried out, because I heard the panic in my own voice. Finley touched my hair. "Don't move. I'll see what happened."

He disappeared into the back of the house. Cinnamon roused at the noise, too. She lumbered over to my mattress and lay down between me and where her master had been sleeping. I petted her absently, my ears straining for sounds of Finley.

At last, he returned. "I have to go outside," he said.

My heart leapt in my chest, every horror story I could imagine springing to life in my sleep-deprived brain. "No," I cried. "It's too dangerous. Wait until morning. There's nothing you can do in the dark."

He crouched beside me. "I have to see what happened, Duchess. It's possible we'll have to leave. There's water coming into the house under a wall. I can't take the chance this cottage will collapse on top of us, and I can't assess the damage from inside. I won't be long, I swear."

"Take Cinnamon with you," I urged.

"I doubt she'll want to go out in this."

"I don't care. I don't want you out there alone."

"Fine." He tugged at the dog's collar. It took three tries to get her on her feet, almost as if she had understood our entire conversation. Maybe she did.

When the door closed behind them, I got up and paced. Then—my curiosity mushrooming by the minute—I peeked into the empty guest room. As Finley had said, the back wall of the house was wet. Water trickled from the roofline down and also oozed from the base of the wall.

Whatever caused the sound we heard must have compromised the structural integrity of the house. Poor Cedric. Poor me, for that matter.

There was little time to brood. I had no sooner returned to the other room than the door burst open with man and dog giving a repeat performance of their arrival hours ago.

Finley looked rattled and wet, though there were no visible signs of damage to him, thank goodness.

"Well," I said, kneeling on my mattress, "what was it?"

By the time he climbed back into bed, the dog was already asleep again. "Not a landslide exactly. Some rocks came tumbling down the hill.

One of them was big, really big. I think it may have damaged the roof and cracked the wall. I can't tell until daylight."

"Is it safe to stay?"

"I think so. If anything, it would be even more dangerous to try the drive back to town right now."

"I'm sorry you're in this mess because of me. You should be at home in your lovely house, snug and warm."

He chuckled, reaching out his hand. "Duchess, I've been in worse conditions, believe me. Besides, I wouldn't have been able to sleep knowing you were up here all alone."

"My hero," I teased.

He tangled his fingers with mine. The simple connection sent zings of heat and pleasure all over my body. "We're wide awake now," he pointed out.

"We'd probably be safer if we were closer together," I said primly. "You know. In case of an emergency."

Releasing my hand, he grabbed the edge of my bedding and dragged my mattress toward him. "I *was* a Boy Scout back in the day," he said. Without asking for permission or making a big deal about it, he scooted me across the now-sealed divide and into his arms.

We groaned in unison. I felt as if I had been anticipating this since the first moment I saw him ride up on his motorcycle, ready to be my somewhat cranky knight in shining armor.

I'd been chilled waiting for him to return from outside. Now Finley was a human furnace, warming my body efficiently. One of my legs ended up wedged between his thighs. I felt something long and hard and ready pressed against my hip. I don't think there was any kind of merit badge for this situation.

We were spooned together now, every bit of him embracing every bit of me. It was a most lovely feeling. I determined in an instant that surviving a spent hurricane was a small price to pay for such a reward.

"Finley," I whispered, afraid to break the spell, "will you make love to me?"

Chapter 20

He reared back and stared at me, his gaze narrowed. "I was headed in that direction, Duchess. Don't rush me."

"It's almost morning. I think we should cut to the chase."

"I was wrong," he said soberly, though his eyes danced with humor. "You're not romantic at all. We have a cozy fire and rain on the roof. What's your hurry?"

"Well," I said, pretending to consider the matter, "if the house *does* disintegrate and crush us, I'd like to know we'd done it at least once."

"Done what?" He kissed my nose.

"You know what. Don't make me say it again. I grew up in the South. Women aren't supposed to be pushy."

He chuckled, his hand at my breast. "Push all you want, Duchess. I'm a grown man. I can tell you when to stop."

When he toyed with my nipple, my stupid pajamas suddenly felt like they were strangling me. "Undress me, Finley. Please. Or put out the fire. Your choice."

His painfully slow pace in unbuttoning my top was nothing more than deliberate torture. I needed to bat his hand away and do it myself, but I didn't want him to see my bossy side.

When he bared my chest, I heard his sharp intake of breath. "Lord, Duchess. You've got magnolia flower written all over you. I thought those tales of soft southern skin were exaggerated, but yours is about the smoothest, prettiest thing I've ever seen."

"There's more," I offered meekly. "You know, skin? You're welcome to take a look and compare."

My sexual experience was admittedly limited. Being playful with a man in the midst of intimacy was not something I'd ever experienced. Finley brought out my inner vixen. Either that, or he was just fun to be with…in every way.

After my provocative suggestion, things got serious…really fast. Evidently, Finley's patience wasn't much deeper than mine. Suddenly, he was stripping off my pajama pants, undies, and even my socks. Now I was bare from the waist down.

His chest heaved as he looked at me. "Last chance for second thoughts," he said gruffly, propped on one elbow.

The man's hands were shaking. His eyes glittered with hunger. And yet still, he gave me a way out.

"I know what I want," I said calmly. Rising up on my knees, I shrugged out of my pajama top and let him look his fill. Despite my daring statement, I felt plenty of nerves, though the look in his eyes bolstered my confidence. He gazed at me as if I were the last stop on the way to heaven.

He cleared his throat. "I'm not sure where to start, Duchess. You're a smorgasbord of delights."

"Kissing is nice," I offered.

"It is, at that."

Without warning, he sat up and dragged me into his lap. His fingers tangled in my hair, steadying my head as he found my mouth and kissed me hard. "It's been awhile, McKenzie. Stop me if I go too fast."

Dazed, I tried to decipher what he meant. He wasn't having sex on a regular basis? What was wrong with the women in Portree?

I wanted to tell him there was *too fast* and *not fast enough*. He didn't need my help. The man knew what he was doing. Not only did any desire for conversation fly out the window, I'm not sure I'd have been able to speak, even if I wanted to.

His lips were firm and coaxing, the taste of him as addicting as French champagne. Even so, I wasn't entirely ready to take the final step.

I pulled back…just a hair. "I need to tell you something, Finley."

A pained look crossed his face. "I have protection if that's what's bothering you."

"No," I said, my cheeks hot. "I want you to know I get it."

He frowned. "Get what?"

"I understand where you're coming from. You like your space, and you're happy the way you are. Not in a relationship. Free. I won't make any demands on you, I swear. I'm on vacation. This falls under the category of fun."

"It's not much fun yet," he groused.

I reached up and smoothed a lock of hair behind his ear. "I'm sorry to interrupt your truly stellar foreplay. I wanted to clear the air."

"Has anyone ever told you you're a brat?"

"More than once, unfortunately. I'll be quiet now."

"What if I make you scream?" His grin threatened retribution.

"Finley! Don't say things like that. You're embarrassing me."

He sobered in an instant. "You'd better get over that. By the time the sun comes up, I'm going to know every inch of your body, Duchess. Fair warning."

This time when he kissed me, it was different. Before, he'd been lazy and sweet in his caresses. Now, he was desperate. Not half as desperate as me.

We rolled wildly from his mattress to mine and back again. He smelled like wind and rain and aroused male. I struggled with his clothing. When he was naked, I almost lost my nerve.

Finley Craig was a beautiful man. Unclothed, he was far more intimidating than ever before. Broad, muscled shoulders gleamed with sweat in the firelight. His jaw was tight, his expression hard to read. His chest was a symphony of sleek muscles and tanned skin stretched taut over ribcage and sternum.

At the moment, he had me on my back, my arms pinned over my head with his two big hands. "Damn, Duchess," he muttered. "Where have you been all my life?"

I wasn't going to be swayed by pretty words. I was a grown woman. I had chosen to have sex with an interesting man because I wanted to know what he would be like in bed.

The analytical part of my brain still managed to reason, though barely, pointing out that this scenario could definitely be labeled a fantasy. A gorgeous man. A stormy night. Physical intimacy ratcheting upward exponentially. "I'm glad I met you," I whispered, driven to honesty by the avalanche of emotions that threatened to consume me.

"Fate," he said with a roll of his eyes.

"Make fun if you want," I said. "I can't help it if you showed up when I was in trouble."

"Somebody else would have come along eventually."

Maybe he was telling me not to get attached to him. Too late. I wrapped my legs around his. We were as close as two people could be but for that final joining. "Kiss me again," I demanded. He tasted like sin. Though he was in the dominant position, I was reaping all the benefits. The feeling of helplessness was a turn-on, because I knew that he wanted what I wanted. And soon.

He left me for thirty seconds, no more, and came back ready for action. When he moved between my thighs, I tensed up. I didn't know why. It wasn't as if I was scared of him.

"What's wrong, Duchess?"

I made myself relax. "Nothing. Just nervous. I'm not very good at this."

He kissed my nose. There was something disarmingly sweet about a guy who could be so gentle and teasing when we were both about to go off like rockets. "Who told you that?" he asked.

"Nobody had to tell me. I haven't exactly had guys knocking down my door to hook up. Some women aren't naturally…um…erotic."

"Oh, Duchess." He shook his head as if he were disappointed in me. And we hadn't even done anything yet. "Don't be a clueless blonde. You're the best kind of hot." He nudged his erection against my sex.

I lost my train of thought when all the blood left my brain and moved south. "The best kind?"

"Yeah. Cool and collected and ladylike. Makes guys like me want to get you mussed and flustered." He pressed all the way in and stayed there, giving me a chance to adjust to his size. I didn't have a lot of basis for comparison, but I had definitely graduated to the big-time.

When I could catch my breath, I opened my eyes and found him staring at me with a peculiar expression. "What?" I asked.

I saw his throat move when he swallowed. "Hush, Duchess. I'm trying not to come."

"Oh." I frowned. "That would be disappointing."

He choked out a laugh. His blue eyes were hazy and unfocused. "Hell, I'm sorry, McKenzie." He groaned and finished, leaving me wondering what had happened. I was no femme fatale. I hadn't even gone down on him, for Pete's sake. Yet here we were, me revved and ready to go… Finley heavy and lax on top of me, his breathing labored and his skin hot.

An awkward silence fell after that. He went into the bathroom to clean up. I pulled the sheet and blanket over me. That was the thing about fantasies. They weren't based on reality. I felt hollow inside. Not because Finley had left me behind, but for being a thirty-two-year-old woman who hadn't a clue how to understand the male of the species. His brain or his sex drive. It didn't really matter. Finley was a mystery to me.

When he came back, he was still naked. I had a difficult time looking at all that male magnificence, so I stared past him into the fire. "I suppose we should get some sleep," I said calmly. "Who knows what will happen tomorrow…weather-wise, I mean."

Finley put his hand on my shoulder. "Move over, Duchess."

"There's not room." I didn't want to pretend like everything was okay. I was frustrated and let down.

He joined me under the covers and lifted me on top of him. Putting his hands on both sides of my head, he kissed me long and deep. "Don't worry, my southern belle. I've taken the edge off. This next time is all about you, I swear."

"Next time?" I was turning into a parrot.

He ran his hands over my back and down to my generous butt. "These are the kind of curves that keep men awake at night," he muttered.

Even if he was exaggerating, I savored the compliment. "I'm fine, Finley. Really. I don't always have an orgasm. Let's go to sleep."

"Sorry, Duchess. No can do. My reputation is on the line."

"I won't tell a soul."

He grinned up at me. Even in the dimly lit room, I could see the mischief in his eyes. "You won't have to. I'm going to make love to you until you forget your name. Everyone in town will take one look at your face and know what we've been up to."

I struggled until he released me. He leaned back on his elbows. I wanted to stand, but I was still naked. Instead, I dragged the blanket around my shoulders. "Be serious, Finley. The sun is up. I can't have sex with you in broad daylight. I'm not that kind of woman."

"Daytime sex isn't a crime…not even in Scotland, I promise. Besides, it's so cloudy and gloomy outside you can close your eyes and pretend it's midnight." He grabbed my ankle and dragged me back into reach. "C'mon, honey. You don't have to be shy with me."

"I'm not shy," I protested.

I must not have been convincing, because before I could stop him, he moved me onto my back and started kissing my breasts.

Chapter 21

Finley knew a thing or two about the female body. I'd never really liked losing control, yet he was pushing all my buttons. The rough caress of his tongue on my nipples had me arching my back and moaning. I heard myself and didn't even care that I was putting on a show. I couldn't help it.

Slowly, Finley moved his way down my body. His navel explorations tickled. When he made it still lower to the really interesting territory, I pressed my thighs together, trapping his hand. "That's enough," I said, the words breathless.

The man was hard again...shockingly, incredibly hard. "Open your legs, Duchess. Or I'll have to do it for you."

The carnal mental image of Finley taking my ankles and pulling them apart made me feel faint. I thought I'd been turned on before. That was nothing apparently. Now I was gasping for breath, trembling with the need to come.

He must have sensed my unease, because his expression gentled. "You can trust me, McKenzie. I won't hurt you, I swear. If I do something you don't like, all you have to do is tell me to stop."

Judging by what had happened so far, we'd both be old and gray before I ever uttered that four-letter word. Telling him to stop wasn't the problem. It was me feeling like I was going to shatter into a million shining fragments. I didn't know if I'd be able to put myself back together again.

Swallowing my misgivings, I tried to relax. Though it seemed desperately erotic to spread my legs with him watching, I did it anyway and was rewarded by the look on his face, part exultant, part stunned.

I dug my heels into the mattress and gripped handfuls of the sheet. "I'm ready."

He laughed at me. The infuriating man laughed at me. “Good Lord, Duchess. You’re not bracing for a firing squad. Relax.”

Easy for him to say. I’d never actually had a partner who returned the favor of oral sex. How did I even know I would like it?

In the beginning, he only used his fingers to play with me. That alone was enough to bring me to the brink. He read my body language and drew back at the last minute. “I love watching you,” he said hoarsely. “You see yourself as shy and repressed, but damn, McKenzie, you’re so sensual and natural you make me tremble.”

I was no longer interested in a discourse about my sexual experience. “Please,” I begged. “I can’t bear it. You’re being mean.”

“Not mean, angel. Not at all. I want to give you everything you’ve been missing. The men in your life should have treasured you…cosseted you. I’m trying to erase the sins of my fellow man.”

“Consider them gone.” I put my hand on his taut thigh. “Please, Finley. I want to come with you inside me. I’m so close it won’t take long. Please.”

For one insane moment I thought he was going to say no. It wasn’t that I had any objection to what he was doing with his fingers and his tongue. I needed him so badly, I ached.

My speech must have convinced him. He grabbed his pants and found a second condom. Then he settled between my legs and thrust hard. He held there at the deepest point for interminable seconds. “Next time I want you from behind,” he muttered. “For now, I have to see your face.”

I knew what he meant. Still, I wanted to guard my emotions, my inner self. Finley was having none of that. Everything in my eyes was there for him to read. Nothing new, maybe. A woman infatuated with him.

Never had I given so much of myself to a man. Not only my body, but my soul. I understood suddenly why the charity masquerade balls I had planned and attended were so effective. They allowed for flirtation and seduction without the added danger of vulnerability.

When Finley started to move, I closed my eyes. Seeing him was too much. How did couples ever survive this stripping away of pretense? Man and woman. Yin and Yang. I wanted to scream and dance and run naked into the storm. My climax hit me with the force of the boulders that had crashed down the hill.

One moment I was straining for the peak, the next, I was falling through fire, each cell in my body exploding with joy.

The room was quiet after that. I cried a little bit when we were done. Thankfully, I don’t think Finley noticed.

He kissed me softly, our lips clinging as if unable to give up one last connection. I felt the muted force of his personality like a soft, familiar blanket. Security. Peace. Sometime later, without speaking, he got up and went to the bathroom. I wanted to freshen up as well, though I wasn't sure my legs would work. I felt the same sense of disorientation that occurs after a tragedy, only in my case it wasn't a tragedy at all. Simply a jolting realization that my life would never be the same.

I was almost certainly falling in love with Finley Craig.

Even as I named the truth that filled me with wonder, I grieved. If Finley wanted a woman in his life on any kind of regular or permanent basis, he'd had plenty of opportunities. He was over thirty-five. Women were drawn to him wherever he went. The female sex was ripe for the picking, yet Finley was still single. And apparently very happy in his bachelor state.

When he came back from the bathroom, he added more wood to the fire. Dragging the sheet around my shoulders again, I crawled out of my comfy cocoon. "I think I'll take a shower," I said. And maybe cry like a baby because I had let myself get too close.

He glanced over his shoulder. "Water will be getting cold. Power's off."

I nodded. How had I not noticed? Even with forlorn daylight sifting into the room, none of the lamps were lit. I had specifically left a small light burning in the hallway. Now, the corridor leading to the bedrooms was dark.

Why wasn't Finley talking? We'd committed the unpardonable sin. He and I together had created a morning-after-the-night before with no place to go. Literally.

Once I managed my escape to the small, dated bathroom, I wrapped a towel around my hair to keep it dry and managed a brief lukewarm shower. I was counting on the fact that after I was dressed I would feel better.

When I finished cleaning up, I heard the front door of the cottage open and close, along with Cinnamon's excited barking. Clearly, Finley was taking her out. Perhaps it was my imagination, but from the vantage point of the tiny window high on the wall over the tub, it seemed as if the rain might be slowing down. I hoped so. Not only was the extreme weather endangering lives, it was making things impossibly awkward for Finley and me.

When I was fully clothed and had pulled myself together, I felt marginally calmer. I found Finley in the kitchen scrambling eggs on the propane stove. "Have a seat," he said. "These are almost ready."

I loved scrambled eggs usually. Right now, the thought of it made my stomach heave. Nevertheless, I forced them down. We had tea, but no toast. Leftover scones were a stale substitute that served the purpose of keeping our hunger at bay.

We ate our meal without saying a word. I was a relative novice at this type of situation. I had counted on Finley's sophistication to handle the small talk. Maybe he was always like this in the mornings.

Finally, I couldn't stand the tension any longer. "What are you thinking about?" I asked, cringing inwardly as the needy question left my lips.

He shrugged, stirring his tea with far more attention than the task warranted. "The storm seems to be waning. I want to get back to town and assess the damage. Without phone and internet, Cedric's house might as well be on the moon."

"A bit of an overstatement," I said, "though I think you're right. You and Cinnamon should go while you can."

His head jerked up, dark red staining his cheekbones. Narrowed eyes glittered with displeasure. "If you think I'm letting you stay here, you're insane. You'll move into *my* house," he said, his tone brooking no argument.

"Don't be daft," I said. Sometimes the Scots' expressions were the best. "I've paid the rent here for an entire month. Obviously the cottage didn't cave in overnight. I'll be fine."

"Duchess…"

The warning note in his voice didn't faze me. I was fighting for my life, scared to the bone. Twice in my life, I'd let sex cloud my judgment about men. You might argue that both those times had been a product of immaturity. I was much older now. Wiser.

I could see from his implacable expression that he would drag me out of here over his shoulder if need be. "Fine," I conceded. "The music festival is over. I'll make a reservation at one of the hotels. Will you handle contacting Cedric's relatives to tell them about the damage to his house, or do I need to do that?"

Leaning his chair back on two legs, he studied my face. "What are you afraid of, McKenzie?" Whenever he dropped the *Duchess* and called me by my real name, I knew he had gone from teasing to being straight with me.

"I can't move in with you, Finley. It doesn't make sense."

"You may be loaded, Duchess, but it also doesn't make sense to pay for a hotel room for several weeks when I have a perfectly good guest room going empty."

"Are you offering to accommodate a tourist, or asking me to share your bed?" I had nothing to lose at this point. And I needed to know.

"I'd say that's up to you. Can't we play this by ear?" He examined my face as if he were trying to see inside my head. It was messy in there. No visitors allowed.

"If I move to your house, will you let me hang out with you in your workshop?" I asked. I hadn't known I was going to say that. The subject had been rolling around in the back of my brain from the beginning.

His walls went up. I saw the moment it happened. His face lost all emotion. "I offered you a guest room, Duchess, not free reign."

I wasn't deterred by his brusque tone, because I was beginning to see that his bark was worse than his bite. "Don't you know that when a man is mysterious, a woman invents all kinds of implausible stories about him?"

He stared at me for a long moment. "You should concentrate on your original plan. You're here to see the island. You can do that using my place as a base."

"Would you be interested in playing tour guide?" I goaded him, looking for a response, though I wasn't exactly sure what it was I wanted.

"No, Duchess. You pointed out early on that you've traveled the world over. I think you'll be fine on your own when it comes to exploring Skye."

If I had been a different kind of woman, I could have lured him back into bed in front of the fire. Not only did I lack the necessary skills for that kind of light, sexy invitation, I sensed that Finley was impatient to leave the cottage. I didn't know if it was the situation with me that was causing his restlessness or if he was truly concerned about his house and his adopted hometown.

Either way, I knew he was right. I couldn't stay here. For one thing, I had a severe case of cabin fever. Though Portree was not exactly the big city, at least there would be distractions from the storm.

As for my relationship with Finley—I was in too deep to walk away, even if I had wanted to. In the days to come, I would play tourist while the sun was up. And when darkness fell, I had a pretty good idea of where I would spend my nights.

Chapter 22

We left Cedric's house just after four that afternoon. The skies were still heavy and dark. The rain had slowed to little more than a drizzle. My plan was to drive my rental car and follow Finley back to Portree. Unfortunately, when we went outside to load my things into the vehicle, we found it mired in mud. The force of the rain and the two thousand pounds of metal had not played nice with each other. Only a tow truck would be able to extract me from my predicament. I had no choice but to join man and dog in the rugged Jeep.

Even with four-wheel drive, the steep, ill-kept drive was treacherous. We bounced and rocked our way down to the main highway. Neither of us spoke during the trip. I sensed Finley had things on his mind.

The silence didn't bother me. I was busy thinking and rethinking my situation. It would drive me crazy if I spent every waking moment trying to understand my host. The healthiest course of action would be to carry on with my vacation as I had planned.

What happened behind closed doors when the sun went down would begin spontaneously…organically…or not at all.

We found the town battered but not seriously damaged. Elsewhere in the Highlands had not been as fortunate. We heard of a major landslide and a road closure near Ullapool. The river in Inverness had overflowed its banks in several locations. Most worrisome was the news that a small village on the banks of Loch Ness had been hit hard with flooding.

I recognized the name. Drumnadrochit. It was the location my friend Hayley had chosen as her home base. Even though I was breaking our pact by not waiting until nine, I powered on my phone and left a message. I found that Willow had done the same, including me in the group text.

Sitting on the front steps of Finley's house, with Cinnamon beside me, I felt a wave of homesickness wash over me. I missed Willow and Hayley. They would ground me and keep me from doing something stupid. Wouldn't they?

Or perhaps I was all wrong. Maybe the two of them would tell me to jump into this thing with Finley as wholeheartedly as if it had a future… to throw caution to the wind. All those clichés about diving in headfirst and living a passionate life.

At the moment, I wasn't passionate about much of anything. I'd let the storm and a one-night stand cloud my vision. If I were going to fall in love this month, it was going to be with the Scottish Highlands, and more specifically, the Isle of Skye.

We ended up in town for dinner. Hamish himself greeted us. "Plenty of tables to choose from," he said with a grimace. "No' much of a crowd tonight." He raised an eyebrow at me. "Still goin' around with this carnaptious auld devil?"

I grinned at him. "Carnaptious?"

"Aye." Hamish translated without being asked. "Grumpy, bad-tempered. Irritable. Carnaptious."

"Well, if that's the definition, then yes."

Hamish chuckled. "Have a seat then. I've some prawns so fresh, they'll flirt with your mother."

The proprietor must have been bored. He pulled up a chair and lingered at our table while we ate. The food, like last time, was astonishingly good. Hamish was a self-taught chef, no fancy culinary institutes in his pedigree. His mother and grandmother were both excellent cooks and had nurtured Hamish's love of food and local dishes in particular.

Afterward, with our stomachs full, Finley and I made the climb back up the hill to his house. Tonight there was no urge to linger by the waterfront and enjoy a late summer evening. Everything was wet. Plus, I don't think we were in the mood for chitchat.

It had been a long tiring day, and neither of us had slept well the night before. I was still mentally scrambling for what my answer would be when Finley invited me to his bed. He took the wind out of my sails when he made it clear that there was to be no repeat of our early morning tryst, at least not tonight.

When we reached the front porch, he unlocked the door and stepped aside so I could enter. "I'll take Cinnamon out," he said. "Then I'm going to work in the shop for a couple of hours. I'm in the middle of a big project, and I got behind this week."

Though I was ridiculously hurt, I smiled. "Sounds good. I think I'll have an early night. I'll see you tomorrow."

As I prepared for bed, I wondered if the sex this morning had spooked him as much as it had me. Surely not. Sex was just sex where guys were concerned.

At nine o'clock, I turned on my phone and was relieved to see a message from both my friends. Hayley assured us she was okay. Seeing tangible proof that Willow and Hayley were physically close to me, relatively speaking, was a huge comfort.

It occurred to me I could join either one of them for the three weeks I had left in Scotland. They were most likely well settled in at their respective lodgings. How would I choose?

* * * **

After a night of deep, restorative sleep, I was up and ready early. In the kitchen, I found an empty cup in the sink, but no other signs of Finley. I told myself I didn't care. My itinerary was back on track. I was excited to see what the day had in store.

Finley had offered me the use of the Jeep until the Cedric's rutted lane dried out enough to rescue my rental. I knew how to drive a stick, but maneuvering on the steep hills of Portree was a challenge.

Once out on the open road, I felt much more comfortable. The sun shone bright and warm again. I wished I had the top down on the Jeep. With my pale skin, it was probably for the best.

The first stop on my itinerary was a return visit to Mealt Falls. Taking new photographs of the dramatic cliff with its free-falling torrent of water would challenge my photography skills in terms of the brilliant light and harsh shadows. I didn't let it deter me that a large bus had pulled up just before I arrived.

I was an island in a sea of chattering tourists. I didn't mind. The day was spectacular. The brilliant blue of the ocean reminded me of Finley's eyes.

When I was satisfied that I had captured what I needed, I drove on. At the northernmost end of the island, where the winds whipped across the open moor on the promontory, I paid the small entrance fee and visited the Museum of Island Life. *Museum* was a loose term. Someone had preserved half a dozen crofters' cottages with traditional thatched roofs. I wandered among the various buildings, studying exhibits about farming implements and domestic life and the rigors of existing so very far away from what my contemporaries and I would call civilization.

It was almost jarring to see the handful of cars parked nearby. Without those, I could easily imagine a woman with three or four children at her knee, all smiling as her fisherman husband brought home the day's catch. Or maybe the two of them farmed together, battling the vagaries of the weather to survive.

When I walked back to the Jeep, I climbed in and sat for a bit without starting the engine, gazing out to sea and thinking. There was nothing between me and the horizon but water. Lots of water. To me the ocean was beautiful and awe-inspiring. What must it have been to an islander two hundred years ago?

Did they see the mysterious depths as an enemy to be bested? Or was the water as familiar and ever-present to them as the skyline of Atlanta was to me? I had the luxury of jets and trains and cars to undergird my wanderlust. The Scots who inhabited these modest, almost claustrophobic cottages were trapped by their circumstances. In sickness and in health, they had only each other.

When my stomach began to growl, I headed on my way. The road curved now, back in the direction I had come, though I was a good distance from Portree. I picked a pleasant spot to pull off the highway and climbed out to have my picnic. With the wind, the logistics were difficult. I sat down on a convenient rock and made do.

I'd picked up some modest supplies in the village. The peanut butter and crackers were more than enough to satisfy me. Food came a poor second to the day's adventures.

Inevitably, I thought about Finley. I'd left him a note as a matter of courtesy and indicated I probably wouldn't be back for dinner. I wasn't pouting or trying to make a point. All I was doing was what he had suggested. Making the most of my vacation.

I was glad I had waited for nice weather to do this long loop of the island. I hugged the west coast now. Next on the list was a visit to Dunvegan Castle, purported to be the oldest continuously inhabited castle in all of Scotland. Dunvegan was the clan seat and stronghold of the McLeod chieftains—and had been for over 800 years.

Though there were many beautiful and romantic castle ruins in the Highlands and throughout Scotland, Dunvegan was a well-cared-for gem. I followed the tour guide from room to room, trying to memorize the snippets of history she shared in her thick accent.

In the large dining room, animal trophies stared down from their vantage points high on the walls. Glass-topped cases held smaller treasures. I spent time reading hand-lettered explanatory index cards whose ink had faded over the years. While our guide was answering questions, I spoke to the older man who stood at attention in the doorway.

I surmised his job was to spot any would-be thieves. He was friendly enough when I approached him. An enormous window at the end of the room near him looked out over the inlet bracketing one side of the castle grounds. The old panes of glass were wavy, though, making it hard to focus my camera lens. I wanted to get an atmospheric shot of the shallows where lichen-covered rocks protruded.

To my surprise, the quasi-guard seemed quite sympathetic to my struggles and offered to lift the window so I could position the camera and shoot without interference. As soon as he did so, a welcome breeze swept into the room. On this August afternoon, the rooms were stuffy despite the thick castle walls.

When the house portion of the tour concluded, we were invited to linger and explore the grounds. The Dunvegan gardens were lush and colorful. The scent of newly mown grass mingled with the unmistakable fragrance of warm weather blossoms.

Even though my Atlanta summers were far more humid and sweltering, there was something familiar and universal about the buzzing of bumblebees and the twitter of birds. A few large trees offered welcome shade. I sat down beneath one of them on a concrete bench and closed my eyes. Had the bench been a tad more comfortable, I might have taken a nap.

When I returned to the graveled parking lot, I was yawning. The little village was barely more than a mile away. I'd been told there was a B&B there with a restaurant that served local seafood. I made it a point when traveling to seek out the charming, quirky places that had a passion for homegrown or home harvested, as in the cold waters around Skye. Hamish's establishment was one of those, The Lonesome Shepherd another.

I dined on smoked salmon and sautéed carrots with blueberry crumble for desert. When I finished, I knew my waistband was tighter than when I went in. I didn't regret a single calorie.

Playing tourist distorted time. I'd told myself when the morning began that I had an entire day at my disposal, yet already it was getting late. I didn't want to be driving unfamiliar roads in the dark. I'd already seen how that turned out. Once. Wrecking Finley's vehicle was not on my top ten list of exciting things to do in Scotland.

Resisting the urge to pull off at any scenic overlooks, I pointed the Jeep south and headed toward Sligachan on the A863. Without stops, the miles flew by. Soon I hit the junction with A87 and headed back north toward Portree to complete my wobbly loop. Actually, on the map my route resembled the two chambers of a heart.

There was more to explore in the southern part of the island, the Cuillin Hills in particular. Maybe I could persuade Finley to go hiking with me one day. The area was more remote and not as easily accessed. I'd feel better having a companion for that leg of my adventures.

Though I was tired and ready to be home, my hands gripped the steering wheel tightly in the last few miles. A hotel would have been lonely and impersonal. At least there I wouldn't have to confront the man who had seen me naked yesterday.

Chapter 23

Finley was sitting on the top step of his porch when I drove up. Cinnamon lifted her head, determined it was me, and went back to sleep at his side.

I climbed out of the Jeep feeling grubby and windblown. It appeared as if Finley had showered recently. His dark hair was still damp, and he smelled like the shower gel I had found in my bathroom.

"Did you have a good day?" he asked.

The words were not at all accusatory, but some odd note in his voice brought my defenses up. "It was lovely," I said. "I did the usual touristy things and took several hundred pictures. I'm beat." I hesitated, not quite meeting his gaze. "I think I'll shower and have an early night."

I thought I could slip past him up the steps and disappear into the house. At the last second, he grabbed my wrist and pulled my hand to his mouth. When he kissed the center of my palm, my heart stumbled.

Finley tugged on my arm until I plopped down beside him. He linked our fingers and rested our two hands on his knee. "I missed you today," he muttered.

"I thought you had lots of work to catch up on."

"I did. I do. I still had time to think about you. And the cottage."

I turned my head to find him smiling at me with such heat and determination that it was a very good thing I was sitting down.

"That's nice," I said.

He laughed. "Ah, Duchess. I wonder what you were like as a kid. Were you always so polite?"

"Probably," I muttered. "I knew about soup spoons and hors d'oeuvre forks before I was out of elementary school. My parents put a lot of stock in good manners. They never said no to much of anything as long as I toed the line."

"Sounds like a lot of pressure for a young girl."

I shrugged. "I've learned how to cut loose over the years. After all, I slept with you, didn't I?"

This time I looked out into the darkness, unable to watch his response to my brave taunt. For a long time, he didn't say anything. He didn't let go of my hand, but he didn't say anything.

At last, he sighed. "I hope that's not exactly correct."

"What do you mean?"

"You used the past tense. If I have my way, it's more correct to say you're *sleeping* with me. See the difference? Or have you decided once is enough?"

Once would *never* be enough. Not once or twice or a hundred times. I couldn't tell him that. "I don't think it's entirely up to me." I picked at a small twig that had clung to the hem of my pants. "How am I supposed to know what you want?"

"I want *you*," he said, the words gruff.

A shiver snaked down my spine. "Okay, then. We're on the same page." My hand was sweaty in his. "I really would like that shower."

"As long as you don't change your mind."

"I won't. I'm serious. But first I want to see your workshop."

* * * * * * *

I showered and put on clean clothes and undies. It would have made more sense to get ready for bed. I didn't want to parade around Finley's workshop that way. Instead, I put on my oldest pair of well-washed jeans and a soft baby blue cashmere sweater I'd had since I was in college. The top was a little snug in the boobs now. I still loved it.

The evening was warm enough that I felt okay in bare feet. I knew Finley's workshop had an outer door. I also knew he accessed it from inside the house most of the time, so I didn't think I'd be stepping on rocks and sticks to get there.

We met in the kitchen. He took one look at me and got a funny look on his face. "What?" I asked, frowning.

"You remind me of a calendar pin-up girl from the 1940s...the kind men used to hang pictures of in their lockers and fantasize about when the bombs were falling and they were scared to death."

"Those women would be called chunky by today's standards," I reminded him, not entirely happy with the comparison.

"I'm giving you a compliment, Duchess. Try not to piss me off."

I realized he was dead serious. "I'm sorry," I said. "I've always been a little self-conscious about my…you know…" I motioned halfheartedly toward my backside.

He shook his head, his lips curving in a wry twist. "I never believed that crap about some women not knowing how beautiful they were… until I met you, Duchess. Damned if it isn't true."

We were in uncomfortable territory now. "I'm nothing out of the ordinary, Finley. I've been fortunate enough to have access to high-end cosmetics, good hair care, and flattering clothes. Not every woman is that lucky."

I backed up against the fridge and wrapped my arms around my waist. I would rather he tell me he wanted me. That was easy to understand. I didn't need the pretty words.

"Maybe someday you'll believe me," he said soberly. "I won't press the issue for now. Let's get this workshop thing over with. I don't know why it's such a big deal."

"You're the one who was all secretive," I said, relieved that he was letting the other subject drop. "Besides, I want to see what you do for a living. I've never known a man who builds ridiculously expensive motorcycles."

"You can't appreciate what you don't understand." He gave me a little smile to let me know the patronizing tone was a joke.

I was willing to be taught. More than anything, though, I wanted to know why Finley Craig was so secretive about his work environment.

He led me back through the house to a narrow door that looked as if it went into the hill itself. The previous owner had certainly built a mishmash of rooms and rooftops. If my estimation was correct, the workshop was at least partly underground, with one end of the long rectangular room opening onto the driveway where I had taken Cinnamon for a walk my first night on Skye.

Finley unlatched the door and stepped back to let me enter. For a moment, we stood in pitch-black darkness until he flicked a bank of switches and the room sprang to life beneath multiple florescent fixtures. The flood of illumination was so bright, I had to shield my eyes for a moment until my pupils adjusted.

I'm not sure what I expected. Maybe on some level I wondered if the whole motorcycle thing was a fabrication. After all, I had more than a little experience with men who lied to me.

But no. Finley's job or vocation or hobby or whatever you wanted to call it was real.

I studied my surroundings with intense interest. My host let me look my fill, not intruding in any way. The concrete floor was slick and smooth, the surface painted gray. It was scrupulously clean. Along the four walls, pegboards and hooks organized a myriad of motorcycle parts: handlebars, fenders, seats…not to mention the usual nuts and bolts. In one quick glance I saw more chrome than the time one of my cousins took me to a NASCAR race in Tennessee.

The room smelled nice, a curious mix of paint and oil and lemon soap. However, it wasn't the specifics of the workshop's layout that left me dumbstruck. It was the pictures on the walls. Dozens of them. Large blowups of photographs mounted on foam board.

The places in the pictures looked familiar—maybe images of other spots in the Highlands? Ones I hadn't seen yet? The trees and waterfalls and mountains were pristine. The photographer had captured the essence of nature as cathedral.

I stepped closer to one picture centered over an aluminum workbench. Studying it intently, I began to realize that the trees weren't exactly right. I'd read articles about Highland forestation. Nothing in twenty-first-century Scotland looked so lush and dense. I turned around and stared at Finley. "Where is this?" I asked.

He shrugged, his hands in his pockets, his gaze guarded. "North Carolina. Near Asheville."

Suddenly everything clicked into place. I'd called Finley a man without a country, if only to myself. Apparently it was true. The man was homesick, aching for the mountains where he'd been born and reared. Yet he had voluntarily exiled himself.

No wonder he hadn't wanted me to see his workshop. These pictures told me more about him in one quick glance than if I had asked him a hundred questions.

I held my tongue, trying to understand the man behind this room. He made no move to curtail my explorations, so I continued, stopping only when I came upon a large three-ring binder. In it Finley had collected photos of his handiwork, alongside the clients who had forked over large sums of cash for the privilege of owning one of Finley's motorcycles.

The bikes were unlike anything I had ever seen. They were beautiful. Sleek. Fast. Even in photographs, I could see they were fast.

At last, I hopped up on one of the worktables and swung my legs. Finley had followed me around the room. Now he leaned against the opposite table and stared at me. "Well?"

I shrugged. "The obvious question is why motorcycles?"

Finley picked up a small metal exhaust pipe and twirled it between his fingers. "That's a long story."

"All of your stories are long," I teased. It was the truth. Even so, I wanted to understand the man whose bed I was about to share. The more I knew of Finley, the more I wanted to know. "Tell me. Please."

In his shoulders I noted a degree of tension as if the telling was difficult, even after all this time. "My grandfather Craig died when I was a junior in high school. A massive heart attack. He was playing golf and keeled over. There was nothing they could do for him."

"I'm so sorry."

"I was devastated. Grandpa Craig was my best friend. To lose him so suddenly was like cutting off a limb. He was a larger than life figure—an entrepreneur, a raconteur...a lover of life. I adored him."

Chapter 24

Even now, though he'd lost his grandfather almost two decades prior, I could hear the pain in Finley's voice. "And the rest of your family? How did they react?" I wanted to keep him talking. I had a feeling this was my one and only chance to make sense of the people and events that had made Finley who he was.

"Everyone was shocked. My grandmother died less than a year later. She told me once that losing him had taken the joy out of her life."

"He must have been a very special man." My heart ached in retrospect for the boy on the cusp of manhood who had lost so much.

"Grandpa's passion was motorcycles. He was the one who taught me how to distinguish a Triumph from an Ecossee…a Harley from a Ducati. He knew it all."

"Did he ride much?"

"Not when I was old enough to remember. As a young man, yes… apparently he was a speed demon. But he and my grandmother made an agreement that when he turned fifty-five, he would give up riding."

"I'm surprised he agreed if he loved it so much."

"You had to know my grandmother. She was an equally powerful force of nature. He worshipped her. When the time came for no more riding, he took it in stride and turned his attention to collecting."

"And you learned at his knee."

Finley grinned. "More or less. I was a head taller than he was when he died. Even though he was only five feet seven inches, you never really noticed that, because he commanded the room wherever he went."

"Was your dad an only child?"

"Yes. So he was the executor of the estate when my grandmother was gone. Grandpa Craig had written out instructions for most of his collection to be sold and the money donated to a particular charity. He left me three of his favorite bikes with the proviso that I could not have them until I turned twenty-one."

"Makes sense. He didn't want you to kill yourself. From what I know of most young men, it takes some time to learn that they aren't invincible."

"I won't argue with that." He chuckled.

"So did you take a celebratory ride on your twenty-first birthday?"

"Not exactly."

"Why not?"

Finley rolled his shoulders and stared at the floor. I felt as if I had tripped over something I didn't see coming. "Never mind," I said quickly. "It doesn't matter."

He lifted his head and stared at me, those gorgeous blue eyes the indigo of a stormy sea. "It mattered a hell of a lot to me. As soon as my grandmother was gone, my father sold every bit of my grandfather's collection, even the three that were mine."

"Oh, Finley. Why?"

"I think he resented the relationship I had with my grandfather, though he would never admit that. He told me the money was far more useful to me in a college fund than tied up in a rich man's toys."

"If you'd been an adult, you could have sued him for not following the specifics of the will."

"True. I had started college by then, and besides, it was too late. The motorcycles were gone. They were the last physical link to my grandfather. Even if I had battled my father, I wouldn't have been able to buy them back."

I was beginning to see that Finley's dad was not a nice person. That's what we used to say in Georgia when we talked about folks we knew who had done something terrible. Now *I* was the one ready to punch somebody. And that somebody was Finley's wretched father.

He had hurt his son deliberately, not once, but multiple times. "Why would he be so cruel?"

"My father is always right. You can ask him, and he'll tell you. All of the things he did to me were for my own good. I was simply the ungrateful kid who didn't understand how fortunate I was."

I flung out my arm, indicating the amazing environment he had created to do the work he loved. "They say the best revenge is living well. I think you've done that, Finley."

It was clear to me now that the reason he kept this place private for the most part was because it revealed so much about him. This was the sanctuary he had created in Scotland. The place he now called home. Would he ever want to go back? Or like the lost inheritance, was it too late?

Closing the small gap between us, I put my arms around his waist and rested my head against his shoulder. “Let’s go to bed,” I said softly. We had shared some heavy stuff tonight. It was time to play.

Finley didn’t take much persuading. “I thought you’d never ask,” he said.

He closed up the workshop, and we went back to my room. I’d left things a mess, so I scrambled to pick up the items I had thrown on the bed. “Sorry,” I muttered. “I was in a hurry.” I felt especially bad now that I had seen his pristine work quarters. The man could do surgery in that room it was so clean.

While I put things away, he picked up a book I had bought at the castle. “Did you enjoy yourself today?” he asked.

I nodded. “I did. Several times in the last two weeks I’ve second-guessed the idea for Hayley and Willow and I to split up here in Scotland. I think it was the right thing to do, though. We’re all three at points in our lives when we’re feeling the need to make some kind of change…or at least to spread our wings.”

“Haven’t you already done that far more than the two of them?”

I’d told him a great deal about my friends, so the question made sense. “Yes. In some ways. Willow is tied to her shop, and Hayley to her classroom. I’ve had more freedom and more opportunities to travel.”

“Then why was it so important to you to strike out on your own in Skye?”

That was a very good question. I was still working on the answer. In the meantime, I could give him a snippet of what I was slowly coming to understand.

“Hayley and Willow have been in my life for a very long time. We’ve been very close as adult women for the last seven or eight years. The problem is, when they look at me, I think they see only one version of me. Does that make sense?”

He flicked the pages of the guidebook, staring at me with that sapphire x-ray vision that made me want to squirm. “If I had to guess, I’d say they were intimidated by you.”

My chin dropped. Hurt coiled in my stomach. “Why would you say that?”

“You’ve got it all, Duchess. You’re smart and incredibly beautiful and charming to anyone and everyone. It must be hard for your friends not to be envious.”

“That’s absurd.”

"It's true. And yes, I agree with you. Though I've never met them, I'll bet they look at you and see a woman who is kind and generous and passionate about standing up for the causes and the people she cares about. What you're trying to tell me is that they don't see your insecurities."

I nodded, my throat too tight to speak.

Finley took my hand and tugged me down on the bed beside him. We sat hip to hip on the edge of the mattress. I watched as he played with the emerald and diamond ring on my right hand.

At last, he sighed. "You were looking for something when you came here, weren't you?"

It must have been a rhetorical question, because he didn't wait for an answer. He kept right on going. "It wasn't Jamie Fraser you were hoping to find. It was McKenzie Taylor—right?"

I swallowed hard. "For a motorcycle jockey, you're awfully damned perceptive."

"Maybe because I struggled with the same thing. Not for the same reasons, of course, but still…" He turned sideways on the bed, taking my face between his hands and looking deep into my eyes. I felt more naked at this moment than at any time I had spent with him in my rental cottage.

"You're making me nervous," I said, trying to lighten the mood.

He kissed me softly on the lips, his mouth moving over mine so sweetly and gently I wanted to burst into tears. When he pulled back, his gaze was no less intent. "You're an amazing woman, Duchess. Whether you're hanging over the edge of a cliff to get a perfect photograph or chasing my crazy dog through the woods or turning me inside out with your enthusiasm for sex, I think you're one of a kind. I hope you find what you're looking for. At the risk of sounding like a cliché, you might discover it was in your own backyard all along."

Some of my warm, fuzzy feelings winnowed away. That wasn't the speech of a man who was toying with any future plans that included me. "Can we talk about something else now?" I begged.

"Like what?"

"Well, how about the fact that you're crazy homesick for the North Carolina mountains. And that you've been in exile for far too long." The only way to deflect his attention from my problems was to focus on his. I could tell from his face that he didn't appreciate the change of subject.

"I love Scotland," he said. "I belong here."

"Maybe you do and maybe you don't. At least I know I'm looking for something. You won't even admit that you need to mend fences with your father."

Wow. I had stepped in it big time.

Finley stood up and walked to the window, his back to me. "I've had my fill of people thinking they know what's best for me. It's my life, McKenzie. My choices. You can either accept that, or I'll leave. You have less than two minutes to let me know, because I really, really want to see what's under that sweater."

The man offered a fair point. I tended to be a fixer, dealing with other people's lives and situations in order to skirt my own issues.

"I'm sorry, Finley. You're right. Let's table the heavy stuff and have some fun."

The relief I felt when he smiled was shocking. I was in over my head in this relationship. Finley hadn't made the slightest indication that we were in the midst of anything other than a vacation fling.

"Stand up," he said.

When I did as he asked, he motioned with his hand. "Start undressing. I'll do the same. We'll see who finishes first."

It was an erotic game of chicken. I unfastened my jeans. He unbuttoned his shirt. Now, I wished I had put on socks and shoes. Footwear would have given me extra leverage in this game of strip poker or strip chicken or whatever we were doing.

When I took off my shirt, I sucked in a breath. I sucked in my tummy, too, just to be sure there was no muffin top on display. My bra was perfectly respectable, not see-through at all. However, the sight of it was enough to make Finley's eyes glaze over.

I heard him mutter a curse. When he shrugged out of *his* shirt, I had to take a step backward. In Cedric's house when Finley and I had sex, the lighting was low. Plus, I'd been shy, so I hadn't spent a lot of time staring. Now I had a full-on view of Finley's chest. It was enough to make a woman go weak in the knees.

We were each bare above the waist. Both of us still wore pants. Finley had a watch on his wrist, one of those huge ones with the fancy dials. Maybe a Rolex. I couldn't tell. If we counted his watch and my bra in the same round, we both had the same amount of items left to remove.

Unless, of course, Finley had gone commando under his jeans. If he had, all bets were off. We stood there gazing at each other with the width of the room between us. The house was quiet.

Wanting him was not a pleasant feeling. It was desperation and vulnerability and uncertainty all wrapped up in a fragile question mark.

I reached behind my back with both hands and felt for the clasp on my bra. “Put the watch on the bedside table,” I said, feigning calm, though I was breathing like a racehorse in the final leg of an important race. “Then we’ll only be one step away from the good stuff.”

Chapter 25

"The good stuff?" Finley snorted and laughed, trying to turn his reaction into a cough when he realized I was serious. "Hell, Duchess. It's *all* been good stuff since you invited me into your bed. But I'll play along."

With exaggerated care, he unfastened his watchband and laid the expensive timepiece aside.

I froze with my arms akimbo like a clumsy crane. "It's really not fair," I pointed out. "I have two volatile locations on my body. You have only one."

He smirked, crossing strong arms over his chest. "That's how we know God's a man."

This seemed like an inappropriate time to discuss theology, so I tried to finish what I had started. Unfortunately, the darn clasp defeated me. My arms prickled with pins and needles from their pretzel-like position behind my back.

Finley took pity on me. "Give up, Duchess. Never send a woman to do a man's job." He kissed the nape of my neck. "You smell good."

I felt his fingers brush my spine as he wrestled with the jammed hook and eye…then a little give in the elastic when he freed me. Reflexively, my hands came up to cover my breasts, holding the bra in place. "Thank you," I said breathlessly. "I can take it from here."

This time his teeth raked the top of my spine. "Why not let me help, sweetheart?" Despite my unspoken objections, he tugged at the bra until I was forced to let it go. I saw him toss it aside. I felt his warmth envelop me when he pulled me into his embrace. "Finley…" I sighed his name like a prayer.

He slid his arms around me. His hands cupped my full breasts. I think we both groaned when he played with my nipples. "Turn around, Duchess. Watch us in the mirror."

I tended to be critical of my naked image. Strangely enough, I didn't look half bad with Finley surrounding me. I bit my lip. "Will you answer a question for me."

He rested his chin on top of my head. "I suppose that depends on the question."

"Why do you think guys haven't wanted to sleep with me?" Once I said it, I was horrified. Did I really mean to unlock all my closets and expose the skeletons?

Finley didn't seem to mind. "There were those two men in the beginning," he reminded me.

"They don't count. I'm thirty-two years old, unattached, and eligible. Nobody asks me out on dates these days."

"Speaking as a guy, I don't know for sure. My guess would be that you scare them. You're out of their league—part ice princess, part movie star."

"Is that what you think?" Given the fact that he was cupping my breasts and pressing his pelvis to my butt, the answer was hopefully no.

"You probably *are* out of my league, McKenzie. I've always liked a challenge."

"Oh, good grief…"

He spun me around in his arms and kissed me hard. "I want you constantly," he complained. "Can't keep my mind on my work. You're a distraction for sure. I wouldn't have it any other way."

I loved what he was saying. I'd never seen myself as a distraction to anyone, much less a man who could probably have any woman he wanted simply by crooking a finger. I thought Scottish accents were sexy. I'm sure the women over here were taken with Finley's American drawl.

"I like you, too, Finley. I didn't think I would. Not after you went out of your way to introduce me to your three friends."

"You deserved it, Duchess. You kept shoving all that Outlander nonsense in my face. Your TV crush Jamie Fraser. Kilts. Muscles. You brought out my fighting instincts."

I cupped his cheek with one hand, feeling the late day stubble on his jaw. "I'll never believe that Finley Craig felt threatened by a fictional hero." I was enjoying our verbal sparring, though I wanted more.

"You forget that I've seen my sister Bella in full-fledged Outlander mode. If she ever met that actor fellow, Sam Heughan, in the flesh, I think she'd probably melt at his feet."

"I don't believe it. Not if she's *your* sister. Any woman who grew up in the same house you did probably deserves a medal for bravery."

Finley tangled his fingers in my hair and tipped my head backward. I shivered. Let him think it was the cool bedroom and not his show of dominance. "I like you this way, Duchess. Bare-ass naked becomes you."

"You haven't even gotten me out of my pants yet, stud."

He gaped at me.

"What?" I said. "A girl can't show a little backbone? You told me I intimidate people. Let's see if I really can. Take off your jeans, Finley. And I'll do the same."

A tiny smile flickered at his lips only to be chased away by a look of masculine determination so intense, I shivered again. Playtime was over.

We separated far enough to step out of our respective items of clothing. In one quick glance, I saw that he wore snug black boxer briefs. He held out his hands. "Satisfied?"

I nodded coolly. "It's a start." Knowing how the evening was likely to end, I had worn my favorite pair of pink satin bikinis. Finley took in every detail. My courage failed after that. I folded my arms across my breasts. "Maybe we should get in bed," I said.

"Because you're tired and want to go to sleep?" His wicked question was accompanied by a knowing smile.

"Because I want to get to know you better…every inch of you."

As unlikely as it seemed, I had surprised him twice in the last few minutes. I was proud of my comeback. It slowed him down long enough for me to climb under the covers.

He caught up quickly. Unlike me, he ripped off his underwear before joining me. He radiated heat. I'd planned to stay on my side of the mattress for a few minutes…long enough to come up with a plan. Finley thought otherwise.

He slid down beside me and dragged me against him. "God, you feel amazing, Duchess. I missed you today."

Those three simple words dissolved my defenses. Did he know that? Was he a pro at saying the right thing at the right time?

What did it matter, really? I wanted Finley.

I was done with talking. I couldn't be rational with his hands on my body. The room was hushed. I could feel my own heartbeat. Or maybe it was his. Against all odds, Finley knew me. My faults. My strengths. My ambivalence about who I was. In being honest with me about his own screwed up life, he had unwittingly given me permission to be myself.

"I'm glad I met you," I whispered. He groaned when I wrapped my hand around his erection. Carefully, I stroked him, learning what he liked, indulging my own curiosity. It was exhilarating. It was fun. This interlude with Finley was destined to be a brief period in my life. I wouldn't let that knowledge take away the joy from this moment.

Unfortunately, the man had his limits. Eventually, he gripped my wrist in a hold that brooked no argument. "My turn, Duchess."

I closed my eyes and stretched my arms over my head, feeling sensual and aroused and happy. Finley didn't care about my money or who my parents or even that I would be leaving at the end of the month. The two of us were in this bed because we wanted each other. It was that simple and that profound.

Finley had perfected kissing as an art form. He started with my lips and charted a slow, lazy course that took him from the pulse at the base of my throat all the way down to the arch of my foot.

I wasn't above begging at the end.

He enjoyed that. A lot.

"Enough," I pleaded. I was hot and shaky and aching to feel him inside me. I sank my fingernails into his shoulders.

His façade of calm and control was only that. His hand trembled as he stroked my collarbone. "I want to make love to you all night, McKenzie. Tell me you want that, too."

"Yes." I closed my eyes, teetering on the brink of a volcanic climax.

He entered me with a steady push. I dug my heels into the mattress and arched my back, determined to take all of him. Instead of feeling hemmed in or pinned down, I gasped beneath a euphoric rush of freedom.

Every cell in my body—every nerve ending—reached for the precipice.

Finley buried his face in my neck. "Talk to me, Duchess. Tell me what you want."

How could he not know? "You," I muttered. "Just you."

He lifted me on top, which meant we were separated for long, frustrating seconds as he rearranged our position. When he entered me again, I winced. I wasn't in the habit of multiple sexual counters in a twenty-four-hour period. My body was tender and a little sore.

Finley watched my face, making me nervous. I didn't mind him enjoying my body. I drew the line at him looking into my psyche. He noticed, of course. "What's wrong, sweet girl? You don't want it this way?"

Something about the position left me feeling painfully vulnerable. "You forgot to turn out the lights. I like the dark."

"So you can pretend I'm a brawny Scotsman?"

I knew he was teasing, but my emotions were raw. "No."

He put his hands on my waist, his tanned fingers a masculine contrast against my pale skin. "We don't need the dark, Duchess. I love watching you. Touch your breasts. Tell me you know how beautiful you are."

It was a lot to ask. Hesitantly, I cupped my own full curves. His gaze was heavy-lidded as he watched. Gradually, I climbed a new level of arousal. Somehow, him watching me touch myself was more intimate than the fact he was lodged deep inside me.

His entire body tensed. This delay in our frantic rush to the end was costing him. Yet still, he didn't move.

I closed my eyes and lightly caressed my nipples. His fingers dug into my hips with bruising force. Encouraged by his reaction, I pressed my breasts together, plumping and squeezing them.

Finley cursed. "Jesus, Duchess. I can't wait."

He rolled me onto my side, lifted my leg over his hip, and pounded into me from behind, shaking the bed and drawing a cry from my parched throat as we strained against each other trying to occupy the same physical space. It was madness and frenzy and deep, unadulterated need.

I wanted it to go on forever. I wanted *us* to go on forever.

When he exploded at the end, hammering into me and groaning as if he were dying, I let go.

With no more inhibitions to stop me, I felt myself fly. My orgasm was intense, draining, and spectacular.

We tumbled together like tired children and slept.

Chapter 26

He made love to me twice more during the night. More importantly, when I awoke the next morning, Finley was still there. He'd been watching me sleep, his head propped on his hand.

I rubbed the corner of my mouth self-consciously, wondering if I'd been drooling. It was a bad time to remember I had never removed my mascara the night before.

"Shouldn't you be working?" I said, glancing at the clock on the wall.

A slight frown appeared between his eyebrows. "Are we going to pretend this never happened?"

"Of course not. It was fun."

The frown deepened. "Have I done something to upset you, McKenzie?"

"Not at all." I winced inwardly at my chirpy tone. "Everything is great."

He reached out and touched my hand…the one that I had unconsciously fisted in the sheet. "Talk to me, Duchess." His tone and his smile were gentle. "Tell me what's going on inside that head of yours."

"I should move to a hotel," I whispered. Everything that had happened was too much, too fast. I didn't have a clue how I was supposed to act, much less any idea of how to protect myself.

He sat up and scraped both hands through his hair. "Sex is not a requirement for staying in my house. I told you that in the beginning. I understand the word *no*, McKenzie."

Stunned, I realized that my awkwardness had wounded him. "I'm sorry, Finley. You're missing my point. I adore being in your bed." *And I adore you.* "I'm afraid if I hang around too long, it won't be easy to leave."

He shrugged. "So stay longer. Your friends could go back on their own."

As an invitation, it lacked a number of details. *Why stay? For how long? Is this a veiled commitment?*

I reached for his hand and rubbed the back of it with my thumb. He had a cut beside one knuckle. "I have to go home," I said quietly. "My ticket can't be changed. I have responsibilities and obligations back in Atlanta."

"What does that have to do with going to a hotel right now?"

Stupid, obtuse man. "I don't want to fall in love with you, Finley. I'm too damn close already. Now do you get it?"

Shock flickered across his face. Men had an aggravating ability to compartmentalize. Sex was easy and simple and soon forgotten. "So you've shifted the romantic fantasy portion of your trip to me?"

I wanted to smack him. He seemed stunned that I would be so blunt. "This isn't a game," I said. "Maybe to you. Not to me. I haven't had a great track record when it comes to men and sex. I suppose I expect too much. I don't want to get my heart broken again. I don't think you have any ulterior motives when it comes to me…it's not that. Still, I'm too old to play around with my emotions."

"I see."

I knew that by putting all my cards on the table I was risking everything, even the short-term pleasure of sharing his bed until I headed for home. "Why don't we take a step back?" I said. "Give ourselves both time to think. I'm not going anywhere today."

"If that's what you want."

When he climbed out of bed, I was treated to a full view of the man in all his glory. I had a sick feeling it would be the last time I'd ever be this close to him. I wanted to grab him and tell him I was an idiot and beg him to come back to bed.

Ironically, Finley had given me the confidence to make the hard decisions. It wouldn't hurt either of us to take stock before we went any farther.

He put on his pants and gathered the remainder of his clothes. At the door, he paused, his back to the room. At the last second, he turned around and stared at me. "What are your plans for the day?"

I lifted a shoulder. "I don't know. If it looks like good weather, I might do some photography here in Portree. Interesting buildings…water shots…that kind of thing."

He nodded. "We could have dinner at Hamish's if you'd like."

The visible peace offering lifted some of the burden on my heart. "That would be lovely."

* * * *

The rest of the day passed in a weird sort of limbo. I spent a number of pleasant hours walking the streets of the charming waterfront town. I had a large memory card in my camera. It was already approaching its limit. Tomorrow I needed to spend some time uploading to my computer and deleting the duds.

Dinner was almost anticlimactic. Finley and I talked about all kinds of subjects. There was no real awkwardness between us, but something had shifted ever so slightly. When we got back to the house, he excused himself to go work in his shop for a couple of hours. I retreated to my room to read and write postcards.

I finally turned out the light at eleven.

Finley wasn't coming to my room tonight. Perhaps never again.

He was an honorable man. Given what I told him about my feelings for him, it made sense that he would call a halt to our physical relationship if he thought I was a temporary fixture in his life.

* * * * * * *

The second morning after I laid my heart on the line, I knew I needed to get out of the house and far away. Physical space might help me sort through my muddled thoughts. I gathered my sturdy walking shoes and sunscreen, preparing to head to the southern part of the island for a hike in the mountains.

After packing a few snacks from the kitchen, enough to hold me until dinner, I grabbed the keys to the Jeep. Finley had made arrangements to have my rental car towed out of the mud and cleaned up, but it wasn't ready yet.

I wasn't exactly sneaking around, though I didn't go out of my way to say goodbye, and I didn't leave a note. Maybe this was for the best. Finley offered me a guest room with no strings attached. It would be up to me to decide if I needed to move on and move out.

When I stepped out onto the front stoop, I nearly collided with a woman wearing a sunshine-yellow sheath reminiscent of Jackie Kennedy. Large dark sunglasses reinforced that notion. "May I help you?" I asked politely. I was eager to be on my way. I knew Finley rarely answered the door during his work hours. Now, the woman knew someone was home.

She seemed taken aback to see me. "Is this Finley Craig's house? Or do I have the wrong address?" The words carried a deep southern accent.

In her presence, I felt like a scruffy teenager. "It is. He's in his workshop right now. You could leave a message."

"And you are?"

Her raised eyebrow made me feel guilty for no good reason. "Just a friend. My name is McKenzie."

She tapped a foot shod in white snakeskin pumps. "I could use your help, McKenzie. It's a matter of life and death."

Apparently, she wasn't joking. Her jaw was set, and I wondered if she had put on the sunglasses to disguise the fact she'd been crying. "What can I do for you?" I asked.

"Will you tell Finley I'm here? He needs to know it's about his father."

I had a very bad feeling about this. "Whom should I say is calling?" Great. Now I sounded like a butler from one of those old movies.

The woman's lips tightened. A muscle ticked in her throat. "Vanessa Craig."

* * * *

It's a wonder I didn't pass out from sheer panic. It's also a wonder I didn't say out loud what I was thinking. *Oh, shit.*

Finley's house didn't have a formal living room. I tucked the lovely Mrs. Craig beside the fireplace and the television. "Please stay here," I muttered. "I'll see if Finley can be interrupted."

It's a good thing I had already been granted access to the inner sanctum, otherwise I think I would have been too much of a coward to bother him. I knocked quietly twice, in case he was in the midst of a phone call. Then I opened the door and peeked in. Finley was standing on the opposite end of the room. A laptop sat open in front of him. Some fancy design program whirled through 3D images of motorcycles.

When he heard me, he dragged his attention away from the screen. "Duchess. What's wrong? Are you ill?"

Was that the only good reason he could think of to justify my trespassing? "No. I'm fine. You have a visitor."

"Tell them I'm busy." His attention drifted back to the laptop. The man definitely knew how to concentrate.

"She's here about your dad. It's important."

Now I had his full attention. His eyes went blank. "Who is it?"

I had trouble saying the word. I knew how much the woman in yellow had hurt him and I didn't want to be the bearer of bad news. I had no choice. "It's Vanessa."

I thought he would take a minute to process. Or even refuse to see her outright. Instead, he brushed past me and went in search of his mother-in-law. When he found her where I had left her, Vanessa stood up. "Hello, Finley."

I was right about the crying. Her eyes were red-rimmed.

Finley didn't acknowledge her greeting. "Is he dead?"

She seemed surprised. "No. Of course not. Bella would have contacted you."

"Then why are you here, Vanessa?"

If Finley had looked at me with that stony gaze, I would have shriveled on the spot. It was possible he was angry, but if so, that emotion was hidden beneath a thick sheet of ice.

Silence reigned as the other woman struggled for words. I tried to feel sorry for her. Knowing what I did of the past, she was on my list of top ten bitches. Sadly, Finley had not lied about her resemblance to me. Vanessa was a slimmer, more sophisticated, slightly older version of me. Actually, it was hard to guess her age. She was definitely older than I expected. Maybe even older than Finley by a few years.

She shot me a look as if wanting to ask me to leave. I started to ease sideways out of the room. Finley took my arm and tucked it through his. His icy calm was preternatural. The man I knew was full of life. Grumpy, sometimes, but vivid and real.

Where my fingers rested on his forearm, the muscles were rigid. He stared her down. "I'll repeat my question. Why are you here?"

Vanessa's hands twisted at her waist. The diamond solitaire on her left hand had to be five carats at least. I couldn't help noticing the way it caught the light. Was that how Mr. Craig senior had lured a younger woman into marrying him? Had he showered her with expensive jewelry and gifts?

At last, she found her voice. "Your father has come to Scotland to make amends with you. I hope you'll meet him halfway."

Finley's lips twisted. "If he's so anxious to see me, why the hell are you here? Since when does my father need to send out a scouting party?"

Grief darkened her eyes. "Since he's been too weak from chemo to get out of bed most days. He's dying, Finley. Your father is dying."

Finley went white under his tan. "Does Bella know?"

"Not yet. He didn't want to worry her. The chemo isn't working. He has a few months at the most, maybe weeks. I wanted to ask you to come home. He said you wouldn't. So here we are. He's back at the hotel. We can go there now if you will."

The naked entreaty on her face almost made me feel sorry for her. Still, my first concern was Finley. "How long will you be here?" I asked quietly. I sensed that Finley was in shock. He would need time to absorb this…both the shock of the visit and the news that his father was on the way out.

Vanessa shrugged. "As long as it takes. You know Donald. He's the most stubborn man on the planet."

"Not too stubborn to die, apparently."

"Finley!" I jerked my arm away, stunned at his callous comment.

Vanessa was less shocked. If anything, her expression carried resignation. "I know how badly we hurt you, Finley. And I deeply regret my part in it. We should have mended the rift long ago. If it makes any difference, I want you to know that I truly love your father."

"Of course you do."

Chapter 27

The situation was deteriorating rapidly.

Vanessa was made of tough stock. She kept going in the face of Finley's disgust. "It's true. I signed a pre-nup. Everything he has goes to Bella. I won't get a cent when he's gone. So please…will you see him?"

The silence built, layer upon layer. I wanted to answer for Finley. *Of course he'll see his dying father.* It wasn't as easy as that.

Vanessa grew impatient. "I need to get back to him. Will you come—"

Finley cut her off with a sharp slice of his hand. "Enough. I need to think about it. I'll call the hotel in the morning and let you know my decision."

I think even Vanessa realized she couldn't push him any farther. "Very well." She picked up her sunglasses and car keys. "I hope you'll do the right thing."

It was up to me to show her out. Finley was a statue, nothing but his blazing eyes suggesting that he was even breathing. Neither Vanessa nor I spoke on the way to the front door. I closed it behind her and leaned against it as my legs gave out.

Shock and tension had combined to turn my stomach and my limbs to jelly. I peeked out the curtain to make sure she was gone. The taillights of her rental disappeared down the drive. Breathing a sigh of relief, I went in search of Finley.

Strangely enough, he had returned to the workshop. I found him in front of his laptop, standing exactly where he had been when I showed up with the news that his ex-girlfriend, now-mother-in-law, wanted to see him.

I hovered just inside the doorway and watched him. "What are you going to do, Finley?"

"If I'm lucky, I'll figure out a way to make this muffler fit into the space I've allotted."

"That's not what I meant and you know it. Don't be snitty with me. Don't shoot the messenger."

"You're the one who let her into my house."

Wow. Apparently that was going to be held against me. "I went outside to leave…practically mowed her over. What was I supposed to do?"

"You could have gone on your merry way. End of story."

"It wouldn't have mattered. She's a woman with a mission. Vanessa would never have left Portree without talking to you."

"This isn't your business, Duchess. Drop it."

"He's dying, Finley. You'll regret it for the rest of your life if you don't make peace with him."

His sharp gaze scorched me from across the room. "How the hell do *you* know what I'll regret?"

I tried to tell myself he was upset. That I should make allowances for his uncharacteristic snarl. His attitude hurt. "Fine. Stay in your stupid, isolated hole in the ground. It's my vacation. I'm going out to have some fun."

* * * ****

The whole day was sucky. Ruined completely, to be exact. I blamed that on Vanessa. The woman was a poisonous snake in my Garden of Eden.

I made myself go for several long walks and take dozens of pictures. Sadly, no amount of gorgeous Highland scenery was going to distract me today. When I finally dragged myself back to Portree, I was hot, rumpled, and depressed.

It didn't take a psychologist to see that Finley wouldn't be so upset if Vanessa hadn't hurt him deeply. Had she destroyed his ability and/or his desire to fall in love?

After I showered and changed into clean clothes, my stomach growled. I didn't know what to do. I had no way of evaluating Finley's current state of mind, and I didn't have the courage to invade his workshop again. Everyone knew it was dangerous to corner a wild animal in its lair.

Finley had transformed from sexy host to wounded bear. I was at a loss as to how I should proceed. I didn't want to walk down the hill and eat alone, so I rummaged in the refrigerator and found some leftover roast beef. Evidently, the housekeeper had been keeping her boss well fed.

Before I could reach for a glass and decide what to drink, Finley appeared without warning. "Where have you been?"

The cranky question was gruff. I counted to ten. "I spent some time in the Cuillin Hills today. Lots of great exercise. Plenty of sunshine. You should try it sometime. Before you turn into a vampire."

Something approaching a smile tilted his lips. "I deserved that." He pulled me close and kissed my cheek before releasing me. "Is there enough of that beef for me?"

"Sure."

I stayed quiet while we ate, not eager to have my head snapped off again. I had spoken my piece. The next step was up to Finley.

He made me wait a very long time. Thirty minutes to be exact. During that time, he consumed three slices of meat, a thick piece of home-baked bread, and two glasses of milk. When he was done, he carried our dishes to the sink. Then he turned his chair around, straddled the seat, and rested his hands, palms down on the table. "You think I'm an ass."

I wrinkled my nose. "Maybe."

He drummed his fingers on the table. "I'm not in love with Vanessa. I never was."

"And yet when she shows up on your doorstep you morph into an evil villain."

"Was I really that bad?"

"Do you want my honest answer?" I gave him a wry smile.

He shook his head. "Okay. I'll cop to overreacting. A little bit."

"A lot."

"You're a hard woman, Duchess. I suppose I owe you an apology."

"Don't knock yourself out."

He reached across the table and grabbed my wrists. "I *am* sorry I hurt your feelings. Forgive me?"

No woman should be expected to resist Finley Craig's blue eyes and sexy smile. Still, I gave it my best shot. "Tell me you're going to see your father in the morning."

The sexy smile faded. Finley let go of me and retreated to his side of the table. "You don't know what you're asking."

"I think I do. He's the monster under the bed. The man who should have protected you and stood by you and instead manipulated you."

"Why do people have to be dying to regret their life's mistakes?"

That was a rhetorical question, so I left it alone.

Finley glowered. "It's emotional blackmail at best."

Still I didn't say anything. I couldn't make him do this.

He paced off the kitchen, over and back. It was a small room, so the circuits were quick. His body language shouted his unease.

At last, he slumped against the wall and scrubbed his face with his hands. "I can't decide this tonight."

It hurt me to see the defeat in his posture. The Finley I'd come to know and love while here in Scotland lived life on *his* terms. Now his past had caught up with him. "Okay," I said. "I'm sorry if you think I've pushed when it's none of my business. I care about you, Finley. And I have something of an objective outside viewpoint. I don't even know your father."

"Will you do something for me?" His eyes were bleak and shadowed.

"Of course."

"Will you let me sleep with you tonight? Just sleep?"

His question took me by surprise. "Of course I will. I think you know it would be more than that."

"Not if I make a promise to you."

I had to smile, despite the bleak situation. "I don't want that kind of promise. We can sleep or make love, or both. I don't think you should be alone tonight. I'm here for you, Finley. In every way."

* * * ***

There was only so much heavy stuff a person could talk about at one time. After my self-revealing statement, we ended up taking Cinnamon for a walk. I felt very much at home in Scotland now, though I knew that my days were numbered. Somehow I had to find the courage to say goodbye to this complicated, sexy, fascinating man.

In the midst of my turmoil, Cinnamon found a dead mouse and dropped it at my feet.

Finley belly laughed at my look of horror. Poor Cinnamon obviously didn't understand why I wasn't praising her. I couldn't even bring myself to stoop and pet her with the mouse at my toes.

"Ick and double ick." Even paradise had its nasty bits.

We walked all the way down the hill and over to the waterfront. I suppose Finley didn't have to worry about running into Vanessa and his father. I assumed they would be eating at the hotel, probably in their room if Mr. Craig was so weak. It said a lot about the older man's motives that he would attempt this trip in his condition.

Was it possible to make up for a decade of bad blood in one week? Or even two? I didn't know. It's true I still remembered the hurtful things my parents had done or not done when I was a child. Everyone wants his or her mom and dad to be perfect. In the end, they're only human. And humans mess up. A lot.

We found the bench where we had spent some time the night of the ceilidh. Cinnamon's leash was long enough for her to play without doing any real damage. The air was cool, but not uncomfortable.

A wave of melancholy swept over me as I counted the days I had remaining. Though I was eager to see Willow and Hayley again, I couldn't imagine walking away from Finley and his adopted hometown.

I would anyway, because that's what grownups do.

Finley bumped my elbow with his. "Penny for your thoughts?"

"There not even worth that," I said. "I was thinking about Willow and Hayley and hoping they've had as much fun as I have."

"You've given them the trip of a lifetime. You're a good friend."

"I hope so. I imagine we'll spend hours when we get home sharing pictures and stories. Soon enough, Hayley will be back at school. I know Willow will be eager to return to her salon."

"And you?"

"Oh, you know," I said with a convincing laugh. "A busy social calendar. Fall in Atlanta is a wonderful time of year."

"You love it there, don't you…?"

"I do. You'd think New York would be a huge draw, and it is. I do enjoy heading north several times a year for Broadway shows and shopping. In the end, though, Atlanta feels like home."

The subject ground to a stilted halt. I imagine both of us were thinking of all those huge photographs in Finley's workshop. Even if he made peace with his father and started going to North Carolina occasionally for visits, he'd built a reputation here in Portree. And a life. I couldn't see him ever going back for good. It wasn't as if he had any interest in running the furniture business when his father was gone. I wondered what would happen to the family company since Bella clearly had carved her own path in the world.

I leaned my head against Finley's shoulder and stared out at the water. If I stayed another month or two, I could make it to all the Outer Hebrides. To tick those islands off the list required plenty of days and planning and adjusting for weather delays. Maybe I could return in the spring.

Somehow, I was going to find the strength to say goodbye without a messy, emotional scene. It wasn't Finley's fault I'd fallen in love. I didn't want him to feel sorry for me. That would be the final blow.

When the time came, I would thank him for his hospitality and ride off into the stunning Scottish sunset, metaphorically speaking.

I should probably go sooner than later, but cheating myself out of the last days I had left was unthinkable. Either way, I was going to grieve.

Either way, I went home without Finley.

Chapter 28

I was yawning when we climbed into bed. Finley was equally subdued. He spooned my back and buried his nose in my hair. "I'm sorry I flipped out today," he muttered. "If I go see him tomorrow. Will you come with me?"

"Yes. If that's what you want." I was surprised he didn't feel the need for privacy. Maybe the thought of facing his father and Vanessa at the same time was too much.

For a long time, we laid there in silence. I thought he had fallen asleep, though I couldn't be sure. I wanted to memorize this moment...crystallize it in some corner of my brain, so I could pull it out on the bad, lonely days and remember what it felt like to be truly happy.

In years to come, I would find another man to love. Finley had restored my faith in that possibility, at least. The idea of children and a home littered with evidence of family life gave my heart a squeeze.

Despite wanting Finley to be the man in the picture, I was under no illusions.

In the midst of my turmoil, I came to a few realizations of my own. I needed and wanted more of a relationship with my parents than I'd had with them thus far. It would require some work on my part. I couldn't expect them to be more than they were. Still, they were blood. One day they would likely be grandparents. In the end, that counted for more than I had ever understood in my selfish youth.

Sighing, I wrestled my pillow into submission and rested my cheek on my hand. Despite the heavy things that had transpired today, I was in the mood for more than snoozing.

"Finley," I whispered, "are you awake?"

Long silence. "Who wants to know?"

His answering whisper made me smile. I wiggled around in his embrace until our noses were practically touching. "I'm sorry you've had a bad day," I said softly. "If it's not too much trouble, do you think you could have sex with me? I know it's an imposition. I can't sleep, and you're better than a tranquilizer."

He huffed. "You're so demanding, Duchess. Don't think I can't hear when I've been insulted. Just for that, I ought to keep you awake all night."

"Promises, promises."

He slid his hands inside my cotton undies and cupped my butt. "The things I do for you," he groaned.

I snuggled closer, feeling his erection nudge my belly. The man might have had a rotten day, but he wasn't dead. I wanted to tell him I loved him. It didn't seem fair to burden him with that. Not now. Maybe not ever. I had let him know where I was headed emotionally. It was up to him to decide what he wanted.

This coming together was different. The same heat was there, though the fire was banked. He wrapped me in tenderness. Every touch of his hands told me he cared about me. Caring and loving were two different animals. I needed to accept what he could give and not beg for more.

I kissed his throat and cupped his sex, inhaling his scent. He was warm and real and so very dear to me already. The few relationships I'd had in the past were pale imitations of this. Scotland had given me my own special man, even if only for a brief moment in time.

"Tell me, McKenzie. Tell me you want this." The words were hoarse.

Couldn't he see the truth? "I want *you*," I said.

He entered me slowly, a firm, steady push. I closed my eyes as little flashes of light spangled the darkness behind my eyelids. Already, my body recognized his. We strained together, him claiming me… me claiming him.

"Ah, God, Duchess." I thought I heard despair in his voice. It wounded me. I didn't want to be another regret in his life. Shoving away the dark thought, I canted my hips and forced him deeper.

We fought each other…ravenous…desperate. I came so hard my head hit the top of the bed. Finley started to laugh. Then he lost control and pistoned his hips. A pained groan ripped from his chest when he found the peace he'd been looking for.

I stroked his back as he fell into the deep, drugged sleep of complete emotional exhaustion. Today had been hard. Tomorrow would be worse.

I lay awake in the dark knowing my decision about the future had changed. I would stay long enough to see Finley through this crisis. Then I would head back to Inverness. Earlier than planned. I'd foolishly thought I could enjoy the time we had left. That was a lie. In the last few minutes, my brain had finally understood what my gut already knew.

Finley was breaking my heart one beat at a time. To stay until the bitter end would be unbearable.

* * * *

In the morning, he was gone…at least from my bed. But this time, there was a note, short and sweet:

I'm going to see him at ten. Meet you in the kitchen. Finley

I waited for the rush of excitement. This was a positive step. Unfortunately, the only emotion I felt at the moment was sadness.

Thinking of Vanessa galvanized me into action. I hadn't worn my white pantsuit since those first three days of the trip. I'd been careful to hang it up, and it was wrinkle free, thank goodness. All I had to do was spot clean a couple of little places on the pants. I chose a lavender silk shell to go underneath and topped it with a white silk Hermes scarf patterned with deep purple irises.

Bringing out the big guns, I clipped platinum hoops in my ears and fastened a matching bangle at my wrist. High heels added the finishing touch. I'd spent so many days lately in casual clothes the shoes felt foreign.

If I were going to be support for Finley, I was going to look the part.

* * * **

None of the hotels in Portree were fancy. Also, none of them were far away. Finley took one look at me, raised an appreciative eyebrow, and picked up the keys to the Jeep. "Clearly we're not walking anywhere with you in those shoes."

I smiled at him and nodded, a little punchy at the effect of seeing him dressed so nicely in khaki slacks, a white button-up shirt, and a tweed blazer. His gaze was clearer this morning. He carried an air of gravity.

The trip took all of ten minutes. We found a parking spot on the street and headed for the hotel lobby. After speaking with the clerk, Finley picked up the house phone and dialed the room.

It must have been Vanessa who answered, judging from what Finley said on his end. When he hung up, he bobbled the receiver of the old-fashioned landline and nearly dropped it. "I guess we'll head upstairs."

I gripped his hand in mine, trying to communicate my concern.

The hotel had a tiny elevator. It was currently in use by a family of four trying to get all of their belongings upstairs in one trip.

"I'll be fine taking the stairs," I said.

We climbed three floors up and stopped in the hallway. Finley's hand was like ice. I leaned into him. "Pretend he's not your dad and that we're just visiting an acquaintance."

His half smile reassured me. "Is that how you get through *your* bad days, Duchess?"

I squeezed his fingers. "Whatever works."

Finley knocked at the appropriate door. Even though we weren't meeting with *my* family, my stomach was in knots. Vanessa let us in. The two-room suite included a modest sitting area. An old man half-reclined in one chair. I felt Finley stiffen in shock.

His father was sallow, his eye sockets sunken. I don't know if he had been bald before. He was now. His age-spotted hand trembled when he lifted it in greeting. "Hello, son."

Finley exhaled. "Hello, Dad."

There was no place for Vanessa and me to go, not that I wanted to abandon Finley anyway. So the four of us sat in an uncomfortable tableau. Vanessa had said her piece up at Finley's house. Now she was mute, her brown eyes worried. She kept looking at Mr. Craig as if afraid he might collapse.

I'm not sure who was expected to break the ice. Finally, thank God, Finley's father jumped in with both feet. "I've come to apologize, son."

"Because you're dying." It wasn't a question.

The old man's shrug was eerily similar to Finley's. "That's one reason. I should have done this ten years ago before you left. But you pissed me off. And it hurt me that you didn't want to take the reins of the company."

Finley leaned forward, his elbows resting on his knees. "It had nothing to do with you in the beginning. I wasn't cut out to be a nine-to-five businessman. I needed more. The kicker was when you sicced Vanessa here on me." He paused and gave both of them a glare. "And when you paid her to seduce me."

The other two people in the room went still. It was clear that everyone except me remembered what had happened in painful detail.

Vanessa finally found her voice. "I should have told him no."

"But there was the fifty grand. Hard to say no to that." Finley's sarcasm made me wince.

His father didn't answer. Vanessa, however, carried the flag. "I admired your father. He was trying to strengthen both companies. The money was an incentive, yes. It didn't seem like such a bad thing he was asking in the beginning. All I had to do was go out on a few dates with you and coax you into seeing the benefits of sticking around."

"And if I had never found out about the money?"

His ex-girlfriend blanched. "Honestly, I felt wrong about what I was doing even in the beginning, but I knew joining the companies was really important. It wasn't like you were in love with me. You were practically still a kid."

"I was twenty-five."

"And I was twenty-nine," Vanessa said. "I should have known better."

Mr. Craig spoke up. "Enough of that. The point is that I hurt you and dragged Vanessa into my mess, too. I want to tell you, Finley, that I'm damn sorry. I've been sorry for a long, long time. I'd like to think you could forgive me, but the important thing is that you know I love you."

Finley's expression was stunned. Had he ever heard that from his father? He was literally speechless.

No one said a word. Finally, sheer nerves made me rush into the breach. "Your son has built an amazing business here in Portree. The town appreciates his contributions and embraces him as one of their own."

Mr. Craig frowned. "And who might you be, young lady?"

Hadn't Vanessa told him about me? Maybe not. Maybe I wasn't worth mentioning. "I'm a friend, sir. Just visiting for a couple of weeks. I came along today for moral support."

Finley stood up suddenly. "This is a lot to take in. I'll come back tomorrow to check on you. Come along, McKenzie. I have work to do."

Before I knew it, we were back outside standing in the sunlight.

Finley's eyes were dazed. "Are you okay?" I asked.

"He doesn't look like the same man. He must have lost fifty or sixty pounds. And she's still with him."

"Maybe she was telling us the truth. Maybe she really loves him."

I could see on his face that was a hard pill to swallow. Having to re-haul his opinions of Vanessa and his father in one fell swoop was a lot to ask.

We drove back to the house in silence. When we arrived, Finley excused himself to go to his workshop. Apparently, someone big and important was due next week to pick up a motorcycle, and Finley was scrambling to finish the order.

I couldn't decide what to do. Most of me wanted to run before I got in any deeper. Still, the thought of abandoning Finley in his time of crisis seemed cold in the extreme.

It looked as if I'd be staying around for at least a short while. I knew it was going to cost me.

Chapter 29

The week following that first painful encounter at the hotel fell into a pattern of sorts. Finley worked in his shop every day until three or so. I spent the same hours playing tourist, searching out little gems I hadn't yet explored, both in town and on the island.

After we cleaned up, we both met in the kitchen around four thirty each afternoon. Most days we walked to the hotel. If the weather was bad, we took the Jeep. We visited with Vanessa and Mr. Craig for an hour or so, shared dinner with them in their suite, and eventually made our way back to Finley's house.

During those visits I learned a great deal about my host. He'd been a daredevil as a kid. Somehow that didn't surprise me. He'd loved sports of all kinds and had broken three bones before finishing middle school.

He and Bella had grieved deeply for their mom when she died. Mr. Craig grieved also, but apparently he'd been unable to let his children see that deep emotion, so they thought he didn't care.

Vanessa and I were mostly spectators. Occasionally she weighed in on subjects concerning Mr. Craig's health crisis and what lay ahead. The specter of death sat in the room with us. Finley's father appeared to have made peace with what was to come.

On what turned out to be our last night with them, Finley squatted beside his father's chair so he could look the older man in the eye. "You need to go home, Dad. Back to your doctors. I'm very glad you came. We'll let the past stay in the past." He paused, and I saw his throat work. "I love you, Dad. I'm sorry I wasn't a better son."

Vanessa cried openly now. Tears stung my eyes, as well. It was hard to watch the sick old man stroke his grown son's hair. Finley's eyes were closed, a look of pained emotion on his face.

Finally, Finley stood. "I'm serious," he said. "You need to go back to North Carolina."

"And will you come to see me?" Mr. Craig straightened, his gnarled hands gripping the arms of the chair.

I think we all knew that making plans like those was an exercise in wishful thinking. I worried that Finley's father might not even survive the trip home.

"Yes," Finley said simply. "Bella and I will make plans. When you get back, you need to tell her the whole truth. You owe her that."

* * * *

That night Finley made love to me only once. It was intense and satisfying, but bittersweet. I sensed the confusion in his soul. There was no way for me to help him. This thing with his father was a road he had to walk on his own.

I lay awake for several hours listening to him breathe. This man. This house. This town. This alluring Isle of Skye. They had conspired against me to steal my soul…my heart…my dreams.

When morning came, I must have been sleeping deeply. Finley was gone… off to work, most likely. Breakfast was out of the question. My stomach churned with nausea.

Carefully, I packed my bags. My rental car had long since been returned to me. It sat outside in the shade, ready for me to load my things. When that task was done, I looked around my bedroom.

Hayley and Willow would ask me about my romantic exploits…or if there had been any. It would hurt too much to open up about this precious time with Finley. Instead, I would be forced to talk mostly about the island itself. That wouldn't be so bad. I had photos and memories aplenty to share with my friends.

At last I was satisfied that I had remembered everything I needed to take with me. I'd spent some time the day before photographing Cinnamon in all her moods. I think I would miss my canine friend almost as much as her master.

Feeling foolish and desperate, I sneaked into Finley's bedroom and looked around for something to put in my silver snuffbox, some memento. On his dresser sat a small wooden bowl, the kind men used for loose change and ticket stubs. I picked up a button that had fallen off one of his shirts. Shoving it deep into my pocket, I scanned the room one last time and shut the door.

I couldn't postpone the confrontation any longer. Wearing my white pantsuit and a smile that was suspect at best, I went to Finley's workshop. When I knocked and entered, he didn't look up. He had grease all over his hands and was finessing something in an engine.

"Hey, Duchess," he said, still concentrating. "It's hot as hell in here today. Would you mind to bring me a beer?"

My throat tightened. "I'll do that before I go."

His hands stilled. Finally, he looked up, and his eyes flashed. Clearly, I wasn't dressed for a day of tromping around the island. "Go where?"

I shrugged. Maybe I had learned that move from him. "It's time for me to go home, Finley."

"I thought you had nine or ten more days."

"Yes. I'm going to spend those in Inverness. It will be fun to explore the town." I didn't tell him I'd already done that once. "Hayley and Willow are going to rendezvous with me a week from Saturday at a little tea shop on Academy Street. I can't believe the days have gone by so quickly."

He wiped his hands on a rag and walked toward me. It took everything I had not to back up. "That's it?" he asked.

His expression was impossible to read. What did he expect from me? The man had never once indicated the two of us were anything more than a pleasant interlude. "You knew when my flight was scheduled." I tried not to sound defensive. I was about to go to pieces, and I didn't want him to see me cry.

"Have I done something to upset you, Duchess?" He looked at me so intently, it felt as if he could see inside my soul.

"Of course not." I summoned a smile. "Why would you say that?"

"So maybe you're still in search of that illusive Scotsman? Hoping to find him in Inverness before your time is up?"

I think he meant the question to be lighthearted. Instead, I heard anger and frustration in his voice.

"You are who you are, Finley. I am who I am. Let's be glad for what we've shared in these few weeks. The situation with your father is going to reach a critical point soon. You'll have to help your sister." I paused. "This thing with you and me was never going to be forever. I knew that."

"Of course," he said. The ice in his words made me flinch inside. "If you'd been more clear about your departure date, I'd have planned a going-away party."

"I didn't decide myself until yesterday. Now that you've made peace with your dad and Vanessa, you don't need me anymore."

Desperately, I wanted him to contradict me. To tell me he loved me. To forbid me to leave.

Apparently, my fairy-tale story didn't end that way.

Finley nodded curtly. "Let me know when you make it to Inverness. So I'll know you're okay." He stepped toward me and kissed me briefly on the lips. "Goodbye, Duchess."

* * * *

I turned and fled. Somehow I made it out of town and took the correct turns. Every emotion was locked down. I clutched the steering wheel and stared at the road, determined not to cause an accident.

Once, I had to stop for a small herd of sheep.

Still my eyes were dry.

At last, I crossed safely over the Skye Bridge and onto the mainland. Not long after, an unlikely moment broke the dam on my tears.

Ahead of me sat the majestic Eileen Donan Castle, settled like an aging queen on a small peninsula in the loch. I hadn't stopped on my trip over to Skye. Once I met Finley, I had counted on him taking me to the castle one day. He said it was a grand idea and promised we'd make the time as soon as the motorcycle was done.

I pulled to the side of the road and let the tears fall.

Something about castles always reminded me of Outlander. I hadn't really expected to find an eighteenth century Scotsman to fall madly in love with me. That was completely illogical.

I certainly hadn't anticipated visiting a stone circle and being whisked back to the 1700s. Everyone knew time travel was a fun idea but highly impractical from a scientific point of view.

So what did I expect from Scotland? And why was I so distraught?

It was my own fault, really. If I had not lollygagged in Inverness that first day, if I had made it to Skye in broad daylight, I would likely never have met Finley Craig. I would have stayed at Cedric's house—bad as it was in the beginning—and ridden out the storm.

I'd told myself I wanted solitude. Instead, I had found love.

The thing about visiting a very old country was that it put things in perspective. How many men and women had walked these moors? How many had faced grief and loss, famine and death? The old world, the time of *Outlander*, was not a forgiving place. A woman's tears were worth very little.

What mattered were the bigger causes.

And yet, against all odds, men and women still fell in love. Somehow I would have to find the resolve to be thankful for my adventure and never to let my two friends see how deeply I'd been hurt during my Highland sojourn.

For the next three days, I checked obsessively with the desk clerk at my hotel for messages. I knew very well that Finley could find me. Days ago he had asked me where I stayed when I arrived from London. Inverness was either a large town or a small city. Any way you looked at it, even if Finley had forgotten the name of the hotel, he would be able to locate me.

Every day he didn't come, I fell deeper into my pity party for one.

After the fifth day, I knew my Highland hero wasn't in love with me… not even a little bit. No amount of pep talks made me feel better. I was desperate for my friends to return, so I could go home and get over this painful chapter in my life.

The Saturday morning of our rendezvous dawned bright and beautiful, worlds away from the dreadful weather that had greeted us upon our arrival weeks before. I checked out of my room and asked the hotel to store my bags until mid-afternoon.

My two friends and I were to catch a three o'clock train back to London where we would spend the night near the station and fly out of Heathrow the following morning.

I made a point of arriving at the cafe early. The lunch menu, though small, sounded delicious. I selected a table, ordered a cup of tea, and sat down with my back to the wall. I didn't want any surprises. If I could see Hayley and Willow coming, I'd be able to compose my expression and greet them with appropriate excitement.

Stirring a single packet of sugar into my cup, I stared down into the warm liquid and told myself I wasn't going to cry. I hated women who blubbered all the time. I was McKenzie Taylor. I had everything in the world a woman could ask for…except Finley. Nobody's life was perfect.

Hayley was the first to arrive. She burst through the door with a huge smile on her face. "McKenzie," she screeched. "I've missed you!"

Feeling her arms close around me took a bit of the hurt away. "I've missed you, too." I hugged her tightly until she protested.

"I have to breathe, silly woman."

Only when we separated did I see the man standing behind her. My eyes rounded. He was gorgeous. Tall and lanky and muscled in all the right places, he also had what looked to be a perpetual tan.

"Introduce me," I said.

Hayley grinned. "This is Angus Munro. I met him in Drumnadrochit. There's more, but let's wait for Willow. I don't want to have to repeat myself."

Fortunately, our missing friend was only seconds behind. She blew into the room with an almost palpable air excitement. Her eyes, usually so guarded, radiated happiness. Behind her strode a tall, extremely handsome, and dignified man. He looked at her with such intense emotion it was almost embarrassing to witness something so intimate.

The three of us women hugged and laughed and hugged again. Then, along with the men, we sat down. I was clearly the fifth wheel.

After the waitress jotted down our orders, Hayley took Angus's hand. "We have some big plans underway," she said. "First I have to go home and teach until they can find my replacement. I can't leave them stranded here at the first of the school year. After that, I'll be moving to Scotland."

"Moving?" My mouth was dry.

Hayley beamed. "Angus is starting a permanent soccer program for kids all over the United Kingdom. He's asked me to used my training and skills to make the school a reality."

Angus kissed her cheek. "And," he said, "important footnote...the lass is going to marry me."

Hayley blushed, all starry-eyed and adorable as we exclaimed and congratulated them.

"Wait a minute," I said. "Munro. That name sounds familiar."

Hayley nodded. "Angus is an internationally famous soccer star."

"It's football," he protested with a pained expression. "And please... I'm just a regular Scotsman these days."

Willow wriggled in her chair. "Is it my turn?"

Chapter 30

Hayley squeezed her arm. "I didn't mean to hog the limelight. Of course it's your turn."

Willow had gained some much-needed weight. I didn't know how else to explain her demeanor except to say she seemed at peace. It was a subtle change, though an important one.

I lifted my voice in order to be heard in the noisy café. "Introduce him, Willow. Please."

She took a breath. "This is Bryce, Laird McBrae. He lives in a castle. I love him."

Bryce grinned, smoothing Willow's hair behind her ear. "What she's trying to say is that our relationship got off to a rocky start, but I won her over with an aging family legacy that's a millstone around my neck."

I lifted an eyebrow. "So *two* weddings on the way?"

Willow shook her head. "No big rush. Bryce has offered to fly my mother and any of you who want to come back over here to Scotland for a destination wedding."

I stared at her in bemusement. Willow, the cynical, hard-working woman with the chip on her shoulder had met a Scottish laird and was going to get married and live in his castle. Maybe *Outlander* wasn't so far-fetched after all.

And Hayley, bookish, earnest Hayley, who barely knew the difference between a pop fly and a home run, was going to marry an elite athlete and teach young children how to play soccer. Maybe I was dreaming.

The two couples began to discuss wedding details, unintentionally sidelining me for the moment. I excused myself and walked up to the counter to add something to my lunch order. It was a flimsy pretext. I needed a moment to breathe.

I was thrilled for my friends, truly I was, absolutely over the moon that this bucket list trip had turned out so well for them. Still, my wounded heart ached so badly, I rubbed my chest.

Had I made a mistake? Should I have stuck around and tried to convince Finley that my love for him was the real thing? That nothing in his past mattered if he and I could be together?

I felt my eyes get hot again. Blinking back the tears, I bit down hard on my bottom lip. There was no way in hell I was going to ruin this moment for my two friends. I had to suck it up and be a mature, rational woman. So what if I was hurting badly? I'd get over it. I always had before…

The clerk handed me my change.

"Since when do you take two sugars in your tea?"

The voice behind me sounded familiar.

I whirled around. "Finley?" I wanted to put a hand on his arm to make sure he was real. I didn't dare. "What are you doing in Inverness?"

He jerked his head toward our table in the back. "Are those your friends?"

I nodded. "Now is not a good time, Finley."

His expression softened. "Don't worry. I won't make a scene. Wait here."

Before I could stop him, he wound his way in between the tightly packed tables and said something to my friends and their significant others.

In unison, all four turned and stared at me.

Finley returned. "We're good," he said. "Let's go outside."

"What did you tell them?"

He steered me out the door and around the edge of the building into a narrow alleyway. Unlike such locations back home, this corridor between streets was decorated with pots of geraniums all along the way. At the moment, Finley and I were the only people present.

"I told them not to go anywhere…that we would be back soon."

"Oh." I stared at my feet.

He bent his head and looked at me. "Aren't you going to ask why I didn't come after you?"

"I know why. You don't love me. You don't want a rich blonde woman in your life." A little of my pique echoed in the words, even though I had tried to speak with dispassion.

"You forgot gorgeous," he said.

"I'm not gorgeous. Vanessa is gorgeous."

Finley lifted his face to the sky. I saw the muscles in his jaw work. "Please don't piss me off, Duchess. I've had a hell of a week."

"Well, boohoo," I cried. "It's not my fault." This time I couldn't stop the tears that welled up and rolled down my cheeks. I dashed them away angrily.

"Oh, Duchess." He folded me into his arms and crushed me against his chest until I could barely breathe. Beneath my cheek, his heart beat rapidly. "I love you, McKenzie. I swear I do. I never even saw it coming."

I pulled back, confused. "What?"

"Cupid's arrow, the fickle finger of fate, my Waterloo. I fell so damned deep and hard I couldn't even find my way back to the surface to breathe. You're everywhere in my house. I took your pillowcases so the housekeeper wouldn't wash them. How pathetic is that?"

"You love me?" I zeroed in on the three words that were most important. "Then why did you let me suffer for over a week? Why did you let me think I was the only one?" I jabbed a finger in his chest. "You broke my heart, Finley."

He tipped back my head and kissed me, long and hard and desperately. Even though I told myself I hated him…or at least I wanted to…I wrapped my arms around his neck and kissed him back. When he finally released me, I had almost forgotten my questions. My lips tingled. My entire body trembled.

Finley shrugged, his eyes shadowed. "Dad died after they landed in North Carolina. I was on a plane immediately. Bella and I planned the funeral with Vanessa. Then there were details…" He wiped a hand across his forehead. "Maybe I should have told you. I don't know. I had a feeling you would insist on flying home with me, and I couldn't interrupt your trip like that. I wasn't thinking very clearly, to be honest."

My brain struggled to catch up. "Your dad died." It wasn't a question. I repeated it, trying to wrap my head around the knowledge. "Bella didn't get to say goodbye." The tragedy of that horrified me.

He shook his head. "She did. Thank God. He collapsed leaving the airport in Asheville. They rushed him by ambulance. Bella made it in time."

"He was conscious?"

"Yes. Briefly. The three of us were at his bedside at the end."

"Oh, Finley. I'm so sorry." I put my arms around him and cried again when he put his head on my shoulder. I held him tightly.

"Thank you," he said, his voice muffled.

"For what? I left you at the worst possible time."

He straightened, his blue eyes sober. "You saved me from making a terrible mistake. If it hadn't been for you, I might never have agreed to see him."

"Nonsense," I said firmly. "I know you, Finley Craig. You would have done the right thing in the end."

"I'd like to think so, but I'm pretty stubborn."

"So was he. You came by it naturally." I pulled a tissue from my pocket and dried my face. "How is Bella?"

"She's okay. Actually, she figured out a long time ago that he was very ill. I did mention that my sister is brilliant, right?"

"Yes. It was still a shock, I'm sure."

"It was." He leaned back against a brick wall, his hands in his pockets. "I told her about you."

"Oh?" I wrapped my arms around my waist, feeling my cheeks heat. "What did you tell her?"

"That you and I had pretty much fallen in love at first sight, but that I had screwed things up by not letting you know how I felt."

"Does she believe in that kind of love?"

"Doesn't matter if she does or not, it's real…isn't it, Duchess?"

My heart started pounding so hard, I felt faint. "You have to be sure, Finley."

His smile made up for all the miserable days. "I'm sure, McKenzie."

"Even so," I said quietly, "this is complicated. I don't have the kind of life that can be easily uprooted. Nor do you."

"I've given that some thought," he said.

"You have?" I was pinballing between exhilaration and sheer panic.

"Lots of people have two homes. Why couldn't we spend six months in Atlanta and the rest of the year here? Could we make that work?"

"Six months away from the heat and humidity? Um, yes. Sign me up for that."

"And we can avoid the Scottish winter by living in balmy Atlanta. Sounds like a win-win."

I nibbled my fingernail, a habit I'd given up years ago. "I don't want you to feel sorry for me, Finley. My falling in love with you isn't your responsibility."

"No," he said soberly. "It's not." He took both my wrists and reeled me in, sliding one arms around my waist and stroking the back of my head with his other hand. "Your falling in love with me is like being anointed with fairy dust. It's the pot of gold at the end of the rainbow. It's that unexpected, unbelievable, bloody amazing feeling of winning the lottery."

I looked up at him, searching his face for the truth. "You really love me? I don't want you to say it if it isn't true."

Without warning, he released me and went down on one knee. The alley was clean as alleys go, but there was no telling what was underfoot.

"Finley," I cried.

He frowned at me. "Hush, Duchess. I'm being romantic." He paused, and I saw him swallow. That he could be nervous stunned me. Reaching in his pocket, he pulled out a turquoise box with a white ribbon.

I sucked in a startled breath. "Where did you get that?"

"Turns out, my return flight to London connected in Atlanta with a four-hour layover. And as it happens…" His grin was pure bad boy.

"There's a Tiffany's in Atlanta." I whispered the words, feeling my legs get wobbly.

Finley untied the ribbon and flipped open the lid. "McKenzie Taylor. Will you marry me? I'm no' a real Scotsman, but I'll love you from this century until the next, no matter where we may be, no matter what life has in store for us. So help me, God."

"Get up," I begged. "We're gathering a crowd." It was true. Passersby had begun to congregate at the end of the alley, sensing drama in their midst.

Finley did as I asked. Taking the ring from the box, he held it out to me. "I won't put it on your finger until you say yes, Duchess."

The ring was the most beautiful thing I had ever seen. A huge Asscher-cut solitaire that splintered the afternoon sunlight and sent it bouncing and sparkling in a million different directions.

"Yes." I had a hard time forcing that single syllable between my lips. I was disorientated and relieved and filled to the brim with incredulous joy.

"Yes, what?"

"I will marry you, Finley Craig. For now, for always."

When he slid the ring onto the third finger of my left hand, we both sighed. It was a perfect fit.

Finley lifted my chin with two fingers and kissed me gently. "Now I suppose I have to call you my Duchess fiancée."

I fretted, even then. "It kills me to think we might have missed each other. What if I hadn't wrecked in that ditch? What if Cedric's house had been perfect in every way?"

He held my hands in his. "I would have found you, McKenzie. I have no doubts at all."

I held out my hand out to admire my new ring. "I suppose we should go back inside and tell the others."

Finley chuckled, holding me close. "I think they already know."

He cocked his head toward the end of the alley. Not only the curious had stopped to stare. Hayley and Angus, Willow and Bryce, had joined the throng.

Hayley waved. Willow blew me a kiss.

My heart was so full I could barely speak. “We did it,” I whispered, so low I don’t think even Finley heard me. “We found our own true loves…”

Be sure not to miss the first book in Janice Maynard's Kilted Heroes series

Hot for the Scot

Read on for a special excerpt from the first book in the series

A Lyrical Shine e-book on sale now.

Chapter 1

On the East Coast train...*somewhere between London and Inverness...*

"Jamie Fraser is a fictional character. Like Harry Potter or Jason Bourne. You're not going to find him wandering around the Scottish Highlands, waiting to sweep you off your feet."

"I *know* that. I'm not delusional. But at least I have a whimsical soul. You wouldn't know a romantic moment if it smacked you in the face."

I listened to the argument with half an ear. Willow, ever the cynic, and McKenzie, the daydreamer, had been hammering away at each other since we left King's Cross. Though we checked out of our hotel and arrived at the train station with plenty of time to spare for our noon departure, McKenzie nearly made us late when she insisted on standing in the snaking line of tourists to get her picture taken at the Platform 9 ¾ sign.

Not only was she a rabid fan of all the Outlander books, she was almost equally smitten with the world of Harry Potter. I couldn't blame her, really. As a primary school teacher and lifelong reader, I'd been called a bookworm and a nerd more than once. My own tattered copy of *Outlander* was tucked inside my backpack, even though my Kindle had enough books to last me until I was old and gray.

I was neither as unique as Willow nor as sophisticated as McKenzie. Middle-of-the-road at best. With the last name *Smith*, the cards were stacked against me when it came to standing out. I spent my days working with women and children and my nights grading papers. My goal for this trip was to live on the edge...to seek out adventure...and to quit being so cautious. I had come to Scotland to find myself.

I suspected Willow and McKenzie had equally private goals, but they hadn't shared them with me. We had all agreed to look for romance. Like Claire Randall, the intrepid heroine of the TV series Outlander, we yearned to find our own down-to-earth but utterly devoted Highlander.

It was a harmless fantasy.

The signposts flying past my window were poetry to me. I'd studied them on the map: Pitlochry, Gleneagle, Lindisfarne. I couldn't wait to leave this train and plunge into the greatest adventure of my life.

Reluctantly, I drew my attention from the passing scenery and intervened before blood was shed. "You're both jet-lagged," I said. "If you're not going to enjoy the trip, at least get some sleep so you won't be grumpy when we get to Inverness. I'm tired of listening to both of you."

We were riding in first class, four motor coach–style seats flanking a small table, two on either side. Lunch had already been cleared away. Our snacks littered the surface between us. So far the cuisine hadn't been all that impressive. But the food was included in our ticket price and better yet, we didn't have to queue up at the meal counter several cars away.

In front of us sat the remnants of our third cups of tea. Or was it the fourth? I'd honestly lost count. Already, I'd made several trips to the tiny restroom at the rear of the cabin. The pleasant stewards passed up and down the aisles, pouring tea and offering cream with almost mechanical precision. At this rate, I'd be a certified Brit by the time we arrived at our destination.

Finally, in response to my schoolmarm glare, my two friends sat back and exchanged sheepish grins, making them look more sleepy than cranky.

Willow yawned. "Tell me again why we didn't fly straight to Inverness?"

"You know why," I said.

Willow wasn't as much of a hard-ass as she liked to pretend. She had a mushy, soft center wrapped in a hard candy shell. Her life had been difficult…much more challenging than mine. I suspected her armor was only skin deep, but it gave her the illusion of being in control.

I opened my notebook. "We agreed that since we can't actually go back in time like Claire does in *Outlander*, this train journey will be symbolic of our desire to go off the grid for a month. No cell phones. No Internet. No Facebook. No Twitter. You agreed, Willow."

"Under duress," she muttered.

McKenzie snickered. "You're bitchy when you're tired."

"And you're even more annoying than usual," Willow drawled.

"Enough," I pleaded. I knew they loved each other. I'd known these two since we all shared a preschool babysitter, my sainted mother. Although the three of us had been a handful even as children, Mom relished the fact that she had two additional daughters in Willow and McKenzie. My parents always wanted a big family, but it wasn't in the cards. I had heard the refrain a million times growing up: *Those two girls are like sisters to you, Hayley. Don't ever let them go.*

But inevitably, I had. In fourth grade, McKenzie's well-heeled parents enrolled her in private school. About that same time, Willow's dad walked out. Willow's mom couldn't keep up with the house payments on her own, so she and Willow had been forced to move all the way to the other side of Atlanta to live with relatives.

I was the one left behind to grow up in the neighborhood where we had spent so many happy times.

Even so, Mom held us together, forcing the exchange of birthday cards and the occasional get-together in downtown Atlanta. By high school, though, the contact between my two childhood playmates and me had become minimal.

Then came Facebook. Mom gleefully searched online for pages of kids she'd shepherded in her daycare. And, of course, she found Willow and McKenzie. Right off the bat, it was apparent that our lives had taken far different tracks. Ironically, I now taught third grade in the elite private school where McKenzie spent most of her grammar school career.

Willow owned *Hair Essentials*, a beauty salon located in a nice middle-class suburb of Atlanta. Her approach to money was save, not spend. It was no wonder she was a little tense. She had taken out a loan against her business to make this trip.

McKenzie had completed an Ivy League education and now filled her days doing charity work with a number of Atlanta-area organizations. She was beautiful and sophisticated and had traveled the world. But underneath it all, she was still the little kid who refused to be afraid of dogs or spiders and wanted to be friends with everyone. I'd always envied her confidence.

Without McKenzie, Willow and I wouldn't be in Europe at all.

Our plan was to stay together tonight at the hotel adjacent to the train station in Inverness. Then tomorrow morning, we would all three go our separate ways. My mood skittered back and forth between exhilaration and terror.

I tapped the notebook where I had underlined the final piece of our plan. "And remember. Every night at nine o'clock, or as close as we can make it, we'll turn on our phones and check for any emergency messages from each other."

McKenzie nodded. “I won’t forget. Willow knows her way around the mean streets, but no offense, Hayley, you’re the one I’m worried about.”

Her remark was fair enough, but it stung nevertheless. “I’ll be fine, McKenzie,” I said automatically. The truth was, I had my doubts. I wasn’t an experienced traveler. Still, McKenzie’s offer had been impossible to resist. She paid for all three of our first-class plane tickets and for three train fares as well. All Willow and I had to cover was lodging and food. Immersing myself in this kind of trip was the opportunity of a lifetime.

McKenzie was Willow’s opposite in almost every way. Her family had money…serious money. Old Georgia wealth that grew even in financial hard times. The impetus for this bucket-list trip was a bequest from McKenzie’s paternal grandmother. Instead of putting her inheritance away for a rainy day, McKenzie decided she wanted to go to Scotland. With us.

Given her background, it wouldn’t be surprising if she were a spoiled brat. But the truth was, she was a sweetheart. A little bossy maybe… and with a tendency to believe she was always right. But a sweetheart. And I loved her.

I loved Willow, too. At the moment, though, I was ready to murder both of them.

Inverness couldn’t get here soon enough…

Meet the Author

Photo by Jamie Pearson Photography

USA Today bestselling author Janice Maynard knew she loved books and writing by the time she was eight years old. But it took multiple rejections and many years of trying before she sold her first three novels. After teaching kindergarten and second grade for a number of years, Janice took a leap of faith and quit her day job. Since then she has written and sold over thirty-five books and novellas.

During a recent trip to Scotland, Janice enjoyed getting to know the "motherland." Her grandfather's parents emigrated from the home of bagpipes, heather, and kilts. Janice lives in east Tennessee with her husband, Charles. They love hiking, traveling, and spending time with family.

Hearing from readers is one of the best perks of the job!

You can connect with Janice at http://www.twitter.com/JaniceMaynard, www.facebook.com/JaniceMaynardReaderPage, http://www.wattpad.com/user/JaniceMaynard, and http://www.instagram.com/JaniceMaynard.

CPSIA information can be obtained
at www.ICGtesting.com
Printed in the USA
LVHW011602020719
623002LV00001B/167/P